ORANGE
COUNTY
CONFIDENTIAL

II

A CHARLIE O' BRIEN PRIVATE INVESTIGATOR MYSTERY

PROFESSOR
ALAN DALE DICKINSON

Orange County Confidential II
Dickinson Publishing Company
By Professor Alan Dale Dickinson

ISBN: 978-1726194105

Chairman of the Board and Chief Executive Officer and Bank Of America, World Corporate Lending Group Vice President And Business Banking Manager (Retired)

P. O. Box 3962
Laguna Hills, CA 92654

A NOTE TO MY READERS

I try to be as factual as possible in my novels, short stories and novellas, however, this is after all, a creative work of fiction. In order to make this subject story ("Orange County Confidential") as interesting, provocative and exciting as possible. I have inevitably taken some artistic (literary) license here and there in this novel, with places, objects, locations, characters, names, and possibly even time.

I trust that my good and very loyal readers will overlook these small author anomalies, a few typo's, and just sit back and 'enjoy' the ride.

DEDICATION

Beautiful, precious and caring, Lynn. She is the sweetest, kindest, most intelligent, thoughtful and well-educated woman that I have ever met in my entire lifetime. She is my inspiration for writing my novels, books, and novellas as well as my reason for living.

PROLOGUE

You have probably heard the old saying (Charlie just loves old sayings, and he uses them all of the time) that all types of dancers and entertainers use all of the time when they are performing, "I am going to bring it all, and I am going to leave it all out on the dance floor."

Detectives, PI's (Private Investigators) and Private eyes, both police detectives as well as private detectives, do pretty much the same things as those listed above. The only difference is that sometimes, just every once in a while, these individuals have to leave some of their own blood and/or lives on the floor (when on their job).

This saying is sort of like Charlie's own personal Mantra (Motto) for his quite dangerous line of work.

PREFACE

One of Charlie's favorite songs:
James Ingram (duet with Michael McDonald, 1985)

"Yah mo B there"

Writers James E. Ingram, Rodney Lynn Temperton, and Quincy Jones
Yellowbrick Road Music, Warner-tamerlane Publishing Corp., and Rodsongs

ONE

CHARLES "CHARLIE" WARNER Kennedy O'Brien (a PI=Private Investigator) awoke with a start (jerk) from his six-month Coma and sat straight up in his bed. He quickly looked around his room, his head felt like it was going to explode, he was quite groggy as if he had the worse hangover ever and he was quite dizzy as well. It appeared that he was in a hospital bed.

He had lots of IV's (intravenous lines) and various tubes, sticking out of his arms and legs and other body parts. Also, he was attached to several very colorful and high-tech looking monitors.

Charlie immediately noticed his very well-educated, and outstanding, GP (General Practitioner) Dr. Anne Elizabeth Ford. She was seated next to his large hospital bed and was reading his personal medical chart. She told him that he was in the 'critical care' ward at the very well respected and excellent St. Jude Medical Center in Fullerton (Orange County), California.

Charlie is one of the few true- life *fearless* Detectives in America or so I have been told. He uses his personal and extensive experience which is based upon his solid daily work ethic and personal beliefs as well as his background of a twenty year career with the LAPD (Los Angeles Police Department) as a Robbery and Homicide Detective, combined with his current ten years of being a PI (Private Investigator, or Private Eye as some prefer to call him), to investigate and then solve, very large 'White Collar' crime cases in the USA as well as all over the Globe.

He finds that by putting his beliefs into action (putting his feet where his mouth is…so to speak) it gives him an edge in understanding, dealing with and then comprehending heinous crooks and criminals of all kinds.

Charlie primarily investigates embezzlement cases in the so called 'too

Big to Fail' Banks in the good ole US of A as well as in foreign countries located all around the world. He also investigates serious criminal activities in 'Ponzi' schemes (think lowlife Bernard L. 'Bernie' Madoff and his 65 *Billion*...yes Billion dollar rip off of the American public). And also, unethical stockbroker/investment bankers (Lehmann Brothers, AIG, JP Morgan Bank, Merrill Lynch [Prior to B of A's purchasing them], Country Wide Funding [one of the worst offenders of all], etc.).

And he also sometimes helps to solve other types of 'criminal' activities that occur in his beloved OC (Orange County, California), where he hangs his hat (lives). Some of these crimes include bank robberies, kidnappings, crooked politician's shenanigans and bombings, just to name a few.

During Charlie's in-depth investigations as a PI, he frequently encounters some very scary villains and heinous and extremely dangerous criminals. He uses his strong and honest beliefs, his devotion to duty, as well as relying on his very sharp mind to assist him in researching and then solving, his very challenging, and complicated, and usually quite dangerous cases.

Dr. Ford said, "Welcome back, Charlie, we missed you." And then gave him one of her quite lovely smiles. Then she added, "Six months ago while you were investigating a criminal case, you were shot by a high-powered M-40 sniper rifle with a high-tech silencer. No one heard the gunshot, for it was as quiet as the whisper of a hunter in the deep forest stalking his prey.

And, no one saw the 'shooter' because he or she was hidden from view in the back of a stolen Chevy Suburban Denali 4 x 4. It had heavy dark limo tinted windows all around. The vehicle had been 'boosted' the night before from a Chevy car dealer at the Irvine Auto Center located just off the 5 Freeway in Laguna Hills, California."

The super hot and fast Denali, had a 454-horse power big block engine for a fast getaway. Charlie has an old saying, "Go Chevy V - 8 or go home." It had large 24" chrome plated wheels with low profile Michelin racing tires.

Also, Dr. Ford told Charlie, the police who were investigating his attempted murder still did not know who had shot him nor why he had been targeted to be taken out (i.e., killed).

Charlie, tried to focus on what she was telling him, he tried real hard and also to cope with the severe and intense pain all over his old body, as well figure out who may have wanted him 'dead instead of alive' when all of a sudden, he was back in La-La Land. Lights out for now Charlie and like Dr. Ford said, "Welcome back, Charlie."

His name is Charles, but his best friends, fellow Private Investigators (Private Eyes), and LAPD (Los Angeles Police Department) Detectives, just call him "Charlie." I want you to know that Charlie does not enjoy getting older. As a matter of fact, he hates it – immensely.

He truly does. People tell him, "Charlie, you look good for your age." He realizes that they are just trying to be kind, however, he wishes that instead, they would say to him: "Charlie, you're still tall, dark and handsome."

That would be a big lie but he would whole-heartedly buy into it. He really would. And, besides, he is still tall, and one-out-of-three isn't bad, right?

He tries and tries, but he just cannot stop good old father time from marching across his handsome (he wishes) face. In addition, most of his previously nice dark black hair is now turning gray. At least he still has all of his hair, thank God! A lot of his friends are bald and they would kill to have gray hair rather than have no hair at all. Oh, well, we all have our crosses to bear in this crazy old world and his currently is that he just does not have the looks, nor the energy, that he did when he was in his prime.

Charlie now lives in Orange County, California (just southeast of downtown Los Angeles) which some people call La-La Land. They are incorrect though, LA is "the City of Angels" it is 'Hollywood' that is really called La-La Land, trust me on that.

He was born and raised here and he most likely will die here...maybe one day soon...you just never know when you will be run over by a big RTD bus or a 400 -horse power Dodge Charger (LAPD police cruiser) chasing a gangbanger in a stolen Mercedes Benz 500S; or even worse, hit by one of the new red-blue-yellow train lines now crisscrossing LA like a scrabble board (or falling dominos).

Then he will go to Heaven he hoped. He actually lives in Newport Beach, California, right on the majestic and royal blue Pacific Ocean. Newport Beach is close to the famous city of Huntington Beach (Surf City, USA).

The other day as Charlie dressed for work, he looked into the mirror. Staring back at him was an extremely handsome angular man, around six feet four with a surfer mop of sun-kissed hair. He had preternatural hazel eyes…so intense that whenever most women looked at him…they had to overt their eyes in embarrassment.

Well, to be truthful, at least his eyes are hazel. He took another look, just for fun, and he saw a good-looking man with an angular face topped by a nest of naturally wavy black hair and a shy smile that made women swoon…so boyish and charming, yet masculine at the same time.

He had a six-pack courtesy of crunches and weight lifting at 24 Hour Fitness and a very strict eating regimen. Then, finally he realized that he was just imagining what he saw in the little mirror. So, he decided to take another look…a harder look this time and he saw his real self, he thought anyway.

Appearing in his mirror was a very nice looking, mature gentleman with a full head of hair, albeit some of it was grey, well all right, a lot of it. With friendly-warm yet piercing hazel eyes, that sometimes looked blue, other times looked green (Irish eyes) and sometimes even looked brown. He did not see a six-pack this time around (frown) nor a smile that would make women swoon, sorry to admit.

All-in-all, what he saw this time was a man who had lived a very hard life, always worked hard, always tried to help others who were less fortunate than himself and always tried to do his best at whatever task he had before him. Then he said to himself, out loud as usual, "Charlie, you are the man!" Then, he turned and left the bathroom with the image of the first man he saw in the mirror, still in his mind's eye.

Charlie fully realizes that he is being *"picayune"*, and he will openly admit it, however, did he ever tell you that he absolutely hates the "Valley" (San Fernando Valley, California). It is located northeast of LA just over the Hollywood Hills with the world famous "Hollywood" sign looking down on the city and the blue majestic Pacific Ocean, along the Ventura Freeway (110-134). Why you may ask is he so down on the Valley?

Well, I shall tell you, the girls and women talk funny out there. Have not you heard of the Valley Girls on TV shows and in the movies?

Also, it gets hotter than Hades out there, up to 110° in the summer time and very humid. In addition, the smog out there (yes, we do have just a little bit of 'grey' air in LA) makes it impossible to breath normally and also it gives you lung cancer.

Last, but certainly not least on his dislike list, is the homes are way overpriced. They sell for about two times what they are really worth. And in some areas, they sell for three or four times more.

Some of the cities that make up 'the Valley' are; Studio City, Burbank, Universal City, North Hollywood, Sherman Oaks, Van Nuys, Sun Valley, Panorama City, Lake View Terrace, Reseda, Calabasas and of course, the City of San Fernando itself, for which 'the Valley' was named.

One of the many cities located in one corner of the Valley, is "Pacoima". It is one of the few areas where the homes are not overpriced as much for some reason. Yes, it is still unbelievably hot, but the girls talk more like music rappers than the rest of the *Valley Girls*. I do not think that they get along that well with each other.

Some people call "Pacoima" a burb (suburb) of LA of about a hundred thousand people. It's major claim to fame during the past one hundred years (century)…besides having a horrendous airplane crash in 1957 that killed several children in a schoolyard…it's Junior High School once taught one of the original founders of "Rock-N-Roll" – singer *Ritchie Valens* (real name Ricardo Esteban Valenzuela-Reyes: (May 13, 1941 – February 3, 1959), singer, songwriter and guitarist). Pacoima Junior High School's name was changed to *Ritchie Valens Middle School* in his memory. Charlie drove by the school by accident last year and it is still there, with no building improvements that Charlie could see, and the hood (neighborhood) around it was still inhabited by honest hard-working lower income families.

A rock and roll pioneer and forefather of the Chicano rock movement, Valens' recording career lasted only *eight* months. During this time, however, he scored several hits, most notably "La Bamba", which was originally a Mexican folk song that Valens transformed with a rock rhythm and beat that became a hit in 1958, making Valens a pioneer of the Spanish-speaking rock and roll movement.

On February 3, 1959, on what has become known as *The Day the Music Died*, Valens was killed in a small-plane crash in Iowa, a tragedy that also claimed the lives of fellow musicians Buddy Holly and J.P. "The Big Bopper" Richardson. Valens was inducted into the Rock and Roll Hall of Fame in 2001.

Ritchie Valens was born in Pacoima, a neighborhood in the San Fernando Valley region of Los Angeles, on May 13, 1941. His parents were Joseph Steven Valenzuela and Concepcion Reyes. Brought up hearing traditional Latino mariachi music, as well as flamenco guitar, R & B and jump blues, he expressed an interest in making music of his own by the age of 5.

He was encouraged by his father to take up guitar and trumpet and later taught himself the drums. One day, a neighbor came across Ritchie trying to play a guitar that had only two strings.

He restrung the instrument, and taught Ritchie the fingerings of some chords. While Ritchie was left-handed, he was so eager to learn the guitar that he mastered the traditionally right-handed version of the instrument.

By the time he was attending Pacoima Junior High School, his proficiency on the guitar was such that he brought the instrument to school and would sing and play songs to his friends on the bleachers.

When he was sixteen years old, he was invited to join a local band named *The Silhouettes* as a guitarist. Later, the main vocalist left the group and Ritchie assumed this position as well.

In addition to the performances with *The Silhouettes*, he would play solo at parties and other social gatherings. Valens was an accomplished singer and guitarist. At his appearances, he often improvised new lyrics and added new riffs to popular songs while he was playing. This is an aspect of his music that is not heard in his commercial studio recordings. Due to his high-energy performances, Valenzuela earned the nickname "The Little Richard of the Valley."

Impressed by the performance, he invited Ritchie to audition at his home in the Silver Lake area of Los Angeles, where he had a small recording studio in his basement. The recording equipment comprised an early portable tape recorder – a two-track Ampex 6012 – and a pair of Neumann U-47 condenser microphones.

Some of them featured drums. These original demos can be heard on the Del-Fi album *Ritchie Valens – The Lost Tapes*. As well as the aforementioned demos, two of the tracks laid down in Keane's studio were taken to Gold Star and had additional instruments dubbed over to create full-band recordings. "Donna" was on track (although there are two other preliminary versions of the song, both available on The Lost Tapes), and the other was an instrumental entitled "Ritchie's Blues."

The first songs recorded at Gold Star, at a single studio session on afternoon in July 1958, were "Come On, Let's Go", an original (credited to Valens/Kuhn, Keane's real name), and "Framed", a *Jerry Leiber* and *Mike Stoller* tune (of the Barry Gordy Motown era).

Pressed and released within days of the recording session taking place, the record was a success. Valens' next record, a double A-side, the final record to be released in his lifetime, had the songs "Donna" (written about his real-life girlfriend), together with "La Bamba."

At this point, in the autumn of 1958, Valens quit high school to concentrate on his career. Keane booked appearances at venues all cross the United States and performances on television programs. Valens, however, had a fear of flying brought on by a freak accident at his Pacoima Junior High School when two airplanes collided over the playground, killing or injuring several of his friends. Valens was not at school that day as he was attending his grandfather's funeral.

He eventually succeeded in overcoming his fear enough to travel by airplane. One of his first stops was Philadelphia to appear on *Dick Clark's American Bandstand* television show on October 6, where he sang "Come On, Let's Go." In November, Ritchie traveled to Hawaii and performed alongside *Buddy Holly* and *Paul Anka*.

Valens found himself a last-minute addition on the bill of legendary disc jockey *Alan Freed's* Christmas Jubilee in New York City, singing with some of those who had greatly influenced his music, including *Chuck Berry*, *Bo Diddley*, The *Everly Brothers*, *Duane Eddy*, *Eddie Cochran* and *Jackie Wilson*. December 27 saw a return to American Bandstand, this time for a performance of "Donna."

Upon his return to Los Angeles, Valens filmed an appearance in *Alan Freed's* movie "Go Johnny Go!" In the film, he appears in a diner, miming his song "Ooh! My Head", using a Gretsch 6120 guitar, the same model Eddie Cochran owned. Still, it isn't Eddie's guitar. In between the live appearances, Ritchie returned to Gold Star several times, recording the tracks that would comprise his two albums.

In early 1959, Valens was traveling the Midwest on a multi-act Rock and Roll tour dubbed "The Winter Dance Party." Accompanying him were Buddy Holly with a new back-up band, Tommy Allsup on guitar, Waylon Jennings on bass, and Carl Bunch on drums; Dion and the Belmonts; J.P. "The Big Bopper" Richardson and Frankie Sardo. None of the other performers had backing bands, so Buddy's backup band filled in for all the show.

After the February 2, 1959, performance in Clear Lake, Iowa, Holly, Richardson, and Valens flew out of the Mason City airport in a small plane that Holly had chartered. He was on the plane because he won a coin toss. The plane, a four-passenger Beechcraft Bonanza, departed for Fargo, North Dakota and crashed shortly after takeoff in a snow storm.

The crash killed all three passengers and the pilot; at 17, Valens was the youngest to die on the flight. The event inspired singer Don McLean's popular 1971 ballad "American Pie" and immortalized February third as "The Day the Music Died".

And, Charlie agreed with McLean, the day that Richie Valens died, the music did die as well, at least a big piece of it. Of course, Charlie felt that the loss of the incredibly talented Buddy Holly, and J.P. 'Big Bopper' Richardson were huge losses too to the rock n' roll world too.

Valens was a pioneer of Chicano rock, Latin rock and was an inspiration to many musicians of Latino heritage at a time when there were very few Latinos in American rock and pop music. He is considered the first Latino to ever successfully cross over into Rock mainstream.

Robert Quine has cited Valens' guitar playing as an early influence on his style. Ritchie inspired the likes of Chan Romero, Carlos Santana, Chris Montez, Los Lobos and Los Lonely Boys. Donna Fox, Valens's girlfriend, is today still recognized as "Ritchie's Donna." Her personalized license plate reads; 'RIPRV'.

Ritchie's nephew, Ernie Valens, has toured worldwide playing his uncle's songs, including a new version of the "Winter Dance Party" tour with Buddy Holly impersonator John Mueller. This tour has taken place at many of the original 1959 venues in the Midwest. Valens is interred in the San Fernando Mission Cemetery in Mission Hills, Los Angeles, California. He has a star on the Hollywood Walk of Fame at 6733 Hollywood Boulevard in Hollywood, California.

In addition to being inducted into the Rock and Roll Hall of Fame, his pioneering contribution to the genre has been recognized by the Rockabilly Hall of Fame. Valens' mother Connie, who died in 1987, is buried alongside him. Valens has been the subject of several biopic films.

Valens was depicted in the 1987 biopic film La Bamba, which was about his life. Primarily set in 1957-1959, it depicted Valens from age 16 to 17. It introduced Lou Diamond Phillips as Valens and co-starred Esai Morales as his older half-brother, Bob Morales. Los Lobos performed most of the music in the film.

Now where was I before I shared Charlie's internet research on the following – 'Ritchie Valens' (a true rock-n-roll pioneer)? Charlie had a lot of free time while he was recovering from his GSW (i.e., gunshot wound) to his head and after he awoke from his six-month coma and was bed ridden for several more weeks afterwards. Dr. Ford told him that he would be released in a few days but to really take it easy until then. And, he should not accept any new private investigator assignments for a few months and not until he was totally recovered. Oh yes, I recall now, Charlie was just about to be released from St. Jude's Hospital in Fullerton in the OC.

TWO

———

AS SOON AS Charlie was released from St. Jude Hospital in Fullerton in The OC (Orange County, California), by his good Doctor Ford, he felt he needed some fresh air, and lots of it. After being in a Coma do to a GSW (gunshot wound), to his skull that almost took his head clean off, for six months, his brain felt like it was full of cobwebs, amongst all kinds of other things.

He decided to take his 'baby' for a ride. His baby was a 1964 Chevy Impala Super Sport with a HO (High Output) V - 8 engine, a four-speed stick transmission mounted on the floor, and special racing rear end. It was maroon with black leather bucket seats. And it was truly a magnificent classic car. Also, it was one of the best Chevrolets ever made in Detroit (Motown).

It was his "weekend set of wheels." He really, really loved this car, and it made him feel young again whenever he drove it. During the week and when 'on the job' he drove one of his two BMW's, either his 535i Gran Turismo Luxury liner with the premium package, satellite navigation system, heated custom-made leather seats and automatic rear shades.

Or he drove his 750i M Sport with executive package, 20 " alloy wheels, active driver assistance, Kardon premium sound system, and a full set of LED lights all around. They were both custom painted with Jet Metallic Black paint, of course.

Charlie drove south on the 5 Freeway (the Santa Ana), to the 133 Laguna Beach Freeway and drove through the absolutely marvelous Laguna Canyon area on his way to Highway One, (the Pacific Coast Highway which runs all the way from The OC to San Francisco).

He stopped in at some very high-end gift shops and a few gorgeous art galleries full of lovely paintings, his favorite Gemologist and Jewelry store in the whole wide world and also the art complex where the "Pageant of the Masters" is held each summer. It has thousands and thousands of people from all over the globe come to see it every year. He has seen it several times himself and loved it.

Then he visited the quite famous and internationally known, "Laguna School of Art" where Charlie knows several of the professors and art scholars who teach there at the Art University. Lots of them are from Paris (The City of Lights), and all over France, and also Roma (Rome) and other parts of Italy, as well as New York City and other famous artist communities all around the world.

Then he proceeded down PCH to the relatively unknown, quite lovely and untouched 'Aliso Park and Beach.'

While Charlie was walking out unto the pier, thoroughly enjoying the scent of the fresh salty ocean air, he spotted a woman lying on her beach towel down below him on the sand. He took off his very expensive custom made Italian black wing tip shoes and meandered down to where she was laying.

As he got closer to her, he immediately noticed she was 'drop dead gorgeous', she really was. She looked to be about 5'9", and had 'great legs', as the men used to say when he was young.

And, her legs were perfectly shaped, toned and very athletic looking, just like the rest of her body. She had a lovely face, and ever so dark brown (almost black) eyes that sparkled in the bright summer sunlight, he noticed when she took off her sexy shades.

She had quite pretty hair, it was an auburn color with red highlights, and even her little nose and ears were cute. Her toe nails were painted red and she had nice feet to go with those nice long legs. She was wearing a very modest yet very attractive royal blue one-piece swimsuit. It just covered her essential body parts, and matched perfectly, with her dark European tan. Charlie was not sure how old she was, but he guessed about 46, or so.

He knew that there are lots of tourists in Laguna Beach and that they come from all over the world to visit this spectacular City and Beach.

Knowing this, he said to himself, "I sure hope that she lives in southern California, and is not just a visitor, so that I may be lucky enough to date her."

She rolled over on her back and said, "Hey, you're blocking the sun for my tan." She already had a fabulous tan, but apparently wanted a deeper one. Then Charlie said, "Oh, I'm so sorry pretty lady, I did not realize that." She then stated, "Are you okay? You look pale and look like you could use some sun yourself." Charlie was stunned by her natural beauty, he truly was.

He noticed she had a slight accent, but could not place where she was from, but definitely not from California. He replied, "Thank you ever so much for your kind comments. I just got out of the hospital today. I was in a Coma for six months and the doctors thought that I was going to die, several times."

Then she responded, "Oh, I feel so badly for you. But I'm very glad that you're out of the hospital and doing much better now." Charlie replied, "Thank you once again pretty lady, in the lovely blue swimsuit, on the beach.

Yes, I do feel 100% better now. By the way, what is your name, if I may be so bold?" She flashed a lovely smile with lots of bright white teeth, which he noticed right away. Then she said, "My name is Lynn Russell."

After which she stood up and Charlie noticed, once again, how sweet and lovely she was. Wow, he said to himself as he certainly did not want to embarrass her. Also, he did not want her to realize how 'smitten' he was with her. She had the figure of a model, very stately, it seemed to him anyway.

Charlie was weak in the knees because of looking and talking to this natural beauty and also, he was still extremely weak 'all over' from his recent six month stay at the Hotel California (he was just kidding, but do you recall the great Eagles song by that name?) he meant the Hospital, of course (i.e., St. Jude Medical Center in Fullerton, California).

Charlie finally did muster up enough physical strength and also the nerve, to invite this lovely creature to dinner at the 'Sand and Surf Resort', a Five Star restaurant in Laguna Beach, just up the road. The restaurant was on pylons built right out over the Pacific Ocean. And, it also had a view of the world-famous Catalina Island to the north.

She had a little beach robe in her car, to cover her fabulous swimsuit and her body, he was sad to see. He loved staring at all of those lovely curves in all of the right places. You know Charlie, always one to appreciate the natural beauties of this world. Then he smiled to himself at that thought.

She was very sweet and asked him since he just got out of the hospital, how much should she spend on her dinner. He replied, "Lovely Lynn, you can order anything that your little heart desires that is on the menu, and please do not worry about the cost." Then he thought to himself, "Also, you can coffee, tea or me, if you would like, for dessert." And then, he smiled broadly again and he was very happy that she smiled right back.

Gazing at this quite lovely natural woman (Lynn), and at the same time looking at the beautiful 'Santa Catalina Island' way off in the distance sitting like floating lily pad in the middle of the gorgeous Pacific Ocean, made Charlie feel like was one of the luckiest men in the OC, and even, perhaps, all of Southern California.

She ordered live Maine lobster which was just flown in from New England according to the pretty young waitress. Also, she asked for the twice baked potatoes with garlic and herbs, freshly picked OC vegetables, imported Italian wheat bread, with Swiss hand churned butter. And, to drink, she wanted Pierre water from France.

Lynn told Charlie that she did not drink soft drinks because they were bad for one's health, and that wine bothered her tummy. And for dessert she ordered Imported New York Cheese Cake. He was still holding out hope that she would order him for dessert later on as well.

He smiled at how his little man brain worked. What she wished for sounded so delicious, that he ordered the same thing, except instead of the cooked veggies, he opted for a fresh Crab Louie salad, with Cesar dressing.

Also, he wanted the NYC chocolate Cheese Cake instead of the original flavor that she got. Everybody who knows Charlie knows he loves, loves, anything Chocolate. He drank milk to sooth his little ulcer friend, and besides 'everybody' needs milk, or so they say in the TV adds.

As they were eating their absolutely delicious lobster dinner, Charlie told Lynn, who was from out of the area (New Jersey), that The OC (Orange County) is one of the loveliest, and eye pleasing, geographical areas in the United States, and maybe even the whole wide world. It also has some of the most beautiful and exquisite beaches anywhere on this Globe that we humans call home, the Earth.

These magnificent beaches are dotted all along The OC as their fingers of white pebble sands reach out and touch the majestic royal blue Pacific Ocean which runs the full length of the Great state of California.

He also told her that one day he would be glad to show her some of these fabulous places and listed a few of the incredibly gorgeous Orange County beaches for her. They were as follows:

LAGUNA BEACH
A. Aliso Beach
B. Irvine Cove Beach
C. Crystal Cove State Beach

NEWPORT BEACH
A. Newport Municipal Beach
B. Balboa Peninsula Beach
C. Newport Dunes Beach

HUNTINGTON BEACH (SURF CITY USA)
A. Huntington City Beach
B. Bolsa Chica State Beach
C. Huntington State Beach
D. Huntington Harbor Beach

CAPO (CAPISTRANO) BEACH
Capistrano Park and Beach

CORONA DEL MAR
(once the home of the famous Ms. Joan Irvine and
long-time home of her quite affluent mother as well)
Corona Del Mar State Beach

DANA POINT
A. Doheny State Beach
B. Salt Creek Beach

SAN CLEMENTE
A. North Beach
B. City Beach
C. Trafalgar Street Beach
D. San Onofre State Beach

SEAL BEACH
Municipal Beach

SUNSET BEACH
A. Surfside Beach
B. Sunset City Beach

Charlie told his extremely lovely dinner companion (Lynn) that he had been to all of these absolutely beautiful, as well as some others, beaches over the years. And that they were all quite lovely (just like her), however, his favorites out of all of them were Aliso Beach in the City of Laguna Beach (where they had just met), Balboa Peninsula Beach in the city of Newport Beach, and Huntington State Beach in the city of Huntington Beach - the adopted home to the Fabulous Brian Wilson and the Beach Boys.

After Charlie left his wonderful dinner date (the lovely Lynn), in Laguna Beach, he jumped back on the 405 (San Diego) Freeway heading north. Then he turned on his custom installed Kardon radio to the Sirus XM radio station. It just so happened that they were playing one of his all- time favorite Classic Rock songs, 'California Dreamin' by the fabulous folk/rock band, the Mamas and the Papas.

He cranked up the volume as loud as it would go and sang along with the group. Luckily no one could hear him, as old Charlie would be the first to tell you that his voice left a lot to be desired, to say the least. Here are the lyrics to that marvelous old tune:

"CALIFORNIA DREAMIN"

All the leaves are brown
(All the leaves are brown)
And the sky is gray
(And the sky is gray)
I've been for a walk
(I've been for a walk)
On a winter's day
(On a winter's day)

I'd be safe and warm
(I'd be safe and warm)
If I was in LA
(If I was in LA)
California Dreamin'
(California Dreamin') on such a winter's day,

Stopped into a Church I passed along the way
(Stopped into a Church I passed along the way)
Well I got down on my knee's
(Got down on my knee's)
And I began to Pray
(I began to Pray)
You know that the Preacher likes the cold
(Preacher likes the cold)
He knows I'm gonna stay
(Knows I'm gonna stay)
California Dreamin'
(California Dreamin') on such a winter's Day.

All the leaves are brown
(All the leaves are brown)
And the sky is gray
(And the sky is gray)
I've been for a walk

(I've been for a walk)
On a winter's day
(On a winter's Day).

If I didn't tell her
(If I didn't tell her)
I could leave today
(I could leave today)
California Dreamin'
(California Dreamin')
On such a winter's day
(California Dreamin')
On such a winter's day
(California Dreamin')
On such a winter's day."

(Written by John Phillips and Michelle Phillips; Publisher Dunhill Records and Lou Adler, 1965).

Wow, Charlie said to himself out loud, what a great song, they just do not make records like the used to 'back in the day.' Charlie is old therefore he prefers the old music to that of today, albeit, he did like some of the newer recording artists. People saw him signing along with the great tune, but luckily for them, they could not hear his off-key voice.

Lovely Lynn had given Charlie her private cell number as well as her personal email. He loved her very dark and mysterious eyes, he really did. Once again, he said Wow, but to himself this time. And then, added, "I am really smitten with this beautiful creature, I really seem to be." Also, he made plans to call her for a date real soon, real soon, indeed.

The quite lovely and ever so charming Lynn made Charlie's heart pump hard, as well as skip a beat (or two or three). Also, she made him feel like he was 6'4" instead of 6'0" tall, and that his IQ (intelligent quotient) was 145 instead of 135 (well above average). And, she made his salt and pepper (well mostly salt these days) hair, turn back to dark black like it used to be.

Charlie will be the first to tell you that even though he is older now (much older), he is still a Hopeful Romantic. Also, he still believes that that the 'love of his life' and his 'soul mate', is out there somewhere waiting for him to find her.

He said to himself, "Charlie do you think that lovely Lynn is that special lady that you have been looking for during the past 15 years?" Then he added another thought, "When a man stops wanting to make love to his wife...he is almost dead.

And, when he quits looking at her nice sensual body, then he is truly dead." He knows that all men all around the world would agree with him, whether they are real- religious or not.

Also, Charlie knew that when he looked deep into the dark and quite mysterious eyes, and at the perfect athletic, European tan and well-toned figure of his pretty new lady friend, that he was neither dead, nor almost dead. He knew that for a fact. He truly did.

After Charlie's best dinner date ever with pretty and very shapely Lynn, he left lovely Laguna Beach and went through the pristine Laguna Canyon Road (133 Freeway) and jumped on the 405 (San Diego Freeway) heading north to his beautiful home right on the water (an inlet from the Pacific Ocean) in Huntington Harbor (i.e., an exclusive area within the Huntington Beach city limits).

He had a boat slip behind his spectacular house and a marvelous 50-foot cabin cruiser (yacht) in his private dock. Charlie just loves to go deep sea fishing off the coast of Cabo San Lucas, or in the Gulf of Mexico. When he is not on the job, of course.

THREE

____

JUST IN CASE that you did not know it, The OC (Orange County, California), is the "Bank Robbery Capital of the World." It used to be LA (Los Angeles, California), up until a few years ago. There are lots of bank robberies all over the rest of the globe, of course, but not quite as many as right here in Southern California.

Charlie was hired as the top Security Operating Officer for '*The Bank of Orange* County.' Their Headquarters was located in the affluent 'Fashion Island' Financial District in lovely Newport Beach, California.

Mr. Thomas Rose was their Chairman of the Board as well as their CEO (Chief Executive Officer). He told Charlie that they had tried everything to halt, or at least slow down, the large amount of robberies that they had over the past two years, but to no avail.

The well-respected Bank had 13 branches located all over The OC. Mr. Rose hired Charlie to an exclusive one year very confidential employment contract and put him in charge of all of the bank's security matters in a last-ditch attempt to put an end to at least most of these robberies.

Mr. Rose was a well-known as well as very respected OC Banker, an active philanphapist, and quite generous supporter of worthy OC organizations. He has a lovely and quite successful career wife, Pamela, who assisted him with his many duties as a Bank Chairman and CEO.

She is a very pretty tall blonde whom always dresses very professionally and has a warm and friendly personality. He also has a sister who had a terrific singing voice and Charlie had heard her sing a few times. Also, she had a very nice family with some real cute little girls.

Thomas was an expert on Banking, Business, Finance and Real Estate loans. The Bank of Orange County has done quite well and grown from

3 to 13 branches during his ten years as the Banks' Chairman. He was a big and strong man and also very athletic, plus he was very well educated and intelligent.

One day about five PM on a Friday night around closing time, Charlie heard an emergency call go out 'over the airways' (Police Frequency), that there was a bank robbery in progress at The Bank of Orange County branch at 4186 Pullman Street, in Costa Mesa.

Charlie was only about five minutes away from there on the 405 (San Diego Freeway) and he had been driving around in between the 13 offices every day now for about two months, just to keep his eyes 'wide open' for possible security breaches and/or potential bank robberies.

Then as Charlie turned the corner, just off of the 55 Freeway and Baker Street and onto Pullman, he saw a brand -new black Chevy Tahoe 4 door SUV. It had paper plates on the rear end, but not real license plates and nothing on the front bumper. It was obvious to him that this was the 'get away' vehicle. It was parked right in front of the bank, in a red 'no parking' zone, with the engine running.

All of the windows were dark limo tinted all around, so that he could not see who was driving the SUV. Then all of a sudden, the driver side window came down and he saw a younger-looking blonde woman, about 25, throw a lighted cigarette out the window and into the street. It almost hit a kid on his bike.

Then, all of a sudden, and out of the blue, Charlie had a frightening Flash Back cross his mind. The very scary obvious bank robbery which was 'going down' and in progress right now and right in front of his old eyes right at this very moment, reminded him of the time that he was wounded and almost killed on February 28, 1997.

That was the occasion when he was an LAPD Police Detective working out of the Robbery and Homicide Division in Van Nuys, California.

That subject event took place at the Infamous North Hollywood bank 'take over' and hostage and hold up, at the 'Bank of America' office located at 6600 Laurel Canyon Drive in North Hollywood in the well-known and famous San Fernando Valley. He recalled 17 people were wounded, plus himself, as well as one customer who was killed in the Fire Fight.

The two idiot perps (perpetrators) who caused all of the havoc and terror that horrible day were:

Larry Eugene Phillips, Jr., born 9-20-1970 in Los Angeles, California and Decebal Stefan Emilian 'Emil' Matasareanu, born on 7-1-1966 in Timisoara, Romania (in Europe).

These two losers met at one of the world-famous *Gold's Gym* in the Valley around 1991. Phillips was a longtime and small-time crook and Con Artist. His father was also a criminal whom lived in Colorado. Emil was a wannabe body builder who had quite inflated aspirations to be the next 'Arnold Schwarzenegger', a weight lifter turned action movie star.

Then, just as quick as that sad and traumatic event popped into his mind, his brain came back to the present and the bank robbery that was in progress right in front of his very eyes.

Charlie checked the 15-round ammo clip in his .40 caliber GLOCK automatic pistol which he always carried with him in his custom-made leather shoulder holster whenever he was 'on the job.' Then he reached down to his ankle holster strapped under his pants and pulled out his .38 caliber Smith and Wesson Police Special five shot revolver.

He wanted to make sure that the .38 was ready to go as well as his Glock. You can never be too careful when going into a possible Gun Fight, Charlie always says. He pulled around the corner and parked out of sight.

He also had a AR-15 Colt semi automatic rifle in the truck of his BMW. He very Nonchalantly took the AR-15 out and put it into a guitar case he kept in his car to hide the rifle. The rifle was compact with a folding stock and the case was small as well. He always carried the big Fire Power for circumstances just like this one that he presently found himself in.

He walked very slowly passed the 'get away' SUV and just glanced inside to see, but he could not with the dark tint, so he just kept walking and entered the bank office. Everything looked normal to a lay person, but to a highly trained professional Private Investigator (and ex-Los Angeles Police Detective) it was not normal at all.

The unarmed security guard was busy flirting with a pretty red-headed woman customer. Charlie immediately spotted the perps and there were three of them.

One was tall 6'4" about 225 pounds, with red hair and quite muscular. The next one was shorter 5'5" about 150 pounds with black hair and a heavy, dark goatee.

And the third bad guy was also muscular, 6'1", with brown hair and around 200 pounds.

All three bad actors (criminals), were white, and they all wore nice form- fitting dark business suits. Charlie, with his very keen eye, could pick them out of a crowd anywhere with their 'criminal demeanor' and the way their eyes kept shifting from left to right, and then back again.

Not to mention they wore expensive athletic shoes, instead of dress shoes, just in case they had to make a 'run for it' and if the 'get away' driver got busted or drove away and left them in a bind.

Charlie immediately grabbed the arm of the Security Guard and told him to Very Discreetly and Quietly get all of the customers out the front door. All three of the perps were near the front of the bank and not look-ing behind them.

That was the job of the getaway driver to watch the front entrance as well as watch for any cops. Also, to listen to the Police Scanner that she had in the SUV and which she was holding close to her ear, for any radio calls to send the police to that particular bank.

Charlie moved like when he was a younger man, and almost like a Ninja Warrior, well maybe not quite that fast. He took cover behind a customer waiting area couch. Then he sent two 'special delivery' .40 caliber Hollow Point bullets into the leg and arm of the crook closest to him, the one with the red hair and the one whom he felt was the biggest threat to him.

He did not shoot 'center mass' (heart), as it looked like he had on body armor. Also, he did not make the 'kill shot' to the head as he wanted the Police to take him alive, if at all possible, so that they could very possibly get some good Intel (intelligence) concerning local holdups in The OC and other helpful criminal-type information.

Immediately, the other two robbers drew their automatic pistols. They both carried Colt 45's (model 1911's) and Charlie knew that gun very well and that it had a lot of Stopping Power, a whole lot. And, he did Not want to get stopped by either of their pistols, Not today anyway.

Then they both fired at Charlie, who was still down and hiding behind the sofa. He counted two shots from each of them, for a total of four. All four lead bullets buried themselves into the couch, and luckily not into Charlie.

Charlie always counted the shots from his own guns as well as his opponents when he was in a gun battle for his Life. That way he would not run out of bullets unknowingly, and also, he would know when his adversaries were low or out of their own ammo.

Next, Charlie shot the smaller and faster 5'5" robber with black hair, as he made a run for the front door to make his escape to the waiting getaway SUV. Charlie shot him in his right foot and his right shoulder.

Once again, he did not want to use kill shots. Then the crook dropped like a 'rag doll' and immediately started yelling for the Paramedics.

The red-headed robber never made a sound after he was shot. He was very tough just like Charlie had guessed that he was. He just lay curled up on the very hard bank tile floor.

Then Charlie noticed the third bad guy with brown hair, who was behind a bank officer's desk that he had turned over toward Charlie for protection from any bullets coming his way.

He looked panicky like a 'caged animal', so he yelled out to Charlie, "If you let me walk out the front door to my SUV, I will not kill you, and I'll let you live to fight the good fight another day. I don't know who you are, man, but you sure are a great shot."

Then before Charlie could respond to his threat, they both heard lots and lots of Police sirens out in the distance and right after that, they both heard the sound of a big V - 8 engine racing and tires screaming, as the blonde getaway driver floored her SUV.

She had decided that she would not stick around and get arrested for attempted bank robbery (a very, very serious Federal Crime), when the cops got there. The hell with her 'partners in crime', they could fend for themselves.

And in just about 60 seconds, she was on the 405 Freeway going 95 miles per hour and weaving in and out of the heavy traffic, on her way to

Tijuana, in good ole Mexico.

Good old Charlie yelled back to the thief, "If you do not surrender, and I mean right this minute, the only way you are leaving this bank is in a 'body bag' and you can take that to the Bank." When the crook did not respond, Charlie thought that he would add, "I am not a cop, and I do not have to take you in alive like they do."

Still no reply, so Charlie took out his M-15 Rifle and sprayed the desk with about 20 to 30 rounds of .223 caliber bullets. Pieces of wood from the desk were flying all over the place. The bad guy decided he did not want to die today, so he yelled to Charlie, "Ok, ok, I give up. You got me."

Charlie rose up from the floor behind the sofa and walked toward him with his AR-15 still pointing right at him. The man stood up and dropped his .45 automatic on the floor and was walking toward Charlie. When he got to about 10 paces from Charlie, he reached into his back pocket and pulled out a .40 caliber Sig-Saurer automatic pistol.

This is a very dangerous weapon and it is used by lots of Police in the USA and also INTERPOL (International Police = the European Police network, located in Lyon, France, just outside of Paris). Charlie felt bad, but he had no choice now, he had given the robber a chance to walk out of the bank alive, but the man did not want to back to prison it appeared.

Then Charlie lit him up like the fourth of July. As he had guessed, all of the crooks had been wearing body armor however the AR-15 with its high-powered bullets perforated his legs, arms, feet, and head. The vest did stop the rounds to his chest area though. Charlie knelt down and then made the sign of the Cross.

He felt very sad that the bank robber did not give up, but he had tried and also, he had just wounded and not killed the other two thieves. You're a good man, Charlie, and you did only 'what you had to do', he thought to himself.

Chapter Prologue: The shortest bank robber with the long black hair pulled back into a pony tail, and dark goatee (whose name was Phillip "Phil" Leonard, Jr.), after his arrest and recovery in the hospital from Charlie's gun shots, told the Orange County District Attorney that Crew of three men and one woman, had robbed ten of 'The Bank of Orange County' offices.

And, he added that they had already made plans to rob the other three remaining branches in the very near future. Also, after they robbed the last three offices, they were going to rob the 'Central Cash Vault' (located in the secure basement) of the Main Office of the Bank in Newport Beach.

And, then he dropped a 'bombshell', a big one, he stated that his girl-friend (Jennifer Marie Whitehead), was the Executive Administrative Assistant to Mr. Rose, the Chairman of the Bank. And, he added, that was where they had gotten all of their crucial bank robbery information, including the staff's routines, locations of the vaults, Brinks Armored Cars delivery dates, times, and so forth.

If our Man, Charlie, had not stopped these vicious Bandits, they would have continued to rob the three offices, the main vault, and quite possibly hurt or even killed several employees and/or customers, the Orange County DA had told Charlie after they had discovered this crucial information.

Charlie said to himself, out loud this time, "If the Border Guards at the Mexican border do not catch the young blonde getaway driver of the black SUV, then I will go to Mexico when I have some extra time and catch her myself (To Catch a Thief, so to speak). No criminal, no one, gets away from old Charlie, at least not for very long."

FOUR

——

CHARLIE GOT A PANICKY phone call late that summer afternoon. The call was from Mr. Joe Johnson, the Finance Manager for the City of Anaheim, California. A Captain at the LAPD (Los Angeles Police Department), had given him Charlie's name and also his unlisted/private cell number. Joe told Charlie that the Mayor Pro Tem for the City of Anaheim, Mr. Donald Bump (whose nickname was Bumpy), was receiving 'Death Threats' in his emails and also the regular US snail (slow) mail.

He had also gotten some very suspicious looking packages VIA Fed Ex, however, Bumpy had not opened those yet because he was worried that they might be IED's or bombs.

Mr. Bump was also on the Board of Directors for the famous *Disneyland* Hotel and Resort and Entertainment Park located in Anaheim. The very honest and competent executive staff at Disneyland (one of the greatest family amusement parks in the whole wide world) would later terminate Mr. Bump when Charlie informed them of the negative results his in-depth investigation. It is the biggest tax payer in the City as well as one of the largest in the State.

He was a very successful Real Estate Broker and also a quite well-known person in the OC. *Everybody* and I do mean everybody in the OC (Orange County), is involved in Real Estate, in one way or another. Either they are a: Broker, Realtor, RE Investor, Property Manager, Own Real Estate Property, or they are currently renting and planning on buying Real Estate in the near future just as soon as they can afford it.

The OC is one of the most expensive Real Estate Markets in all of California as well as the United States. He lived in Lemon Heights, California, a very affluent area located up in the foothills overlooking Anaheim, Tustin, Orange, Santa Ana, Buena Park, as well as the rest of the lovely OC.

The Donald (Mr. Bump) lived with his lovely girlfriend, Ms. Linda Bertolli. She was a former Pasadena Rose Parade Queen, as well as the first runner up for the Miss California Beauty Pageant and crown. He was 65 years old and she was 35. He was short, 5'5", bald, and about 250 pounds.

She was 'gorgeous beyond belief' at 5'9" and 135 pounds, and measured 36-24-36 with long, down to her bottom straight fire engine Red hair. Also, she had very striking crystal blue eyes and she would bring Tears to the eyes of most happily married men.

Joe wanted Charlie to find the perp (perpetrator) and criminal, behind the Death Threats, and then have him or her, arrested by the Anaheim Police Department, or the Orange County Sheriff's Department, depending upon whose jurisdiction they were found in.

The Orange County DA (District Attorney), Mr. John Anderson would be involved too, of course. He had a reputation for being very hard on this type of Hate crimes, as well as crooked politicians, and gang bangers, as such. Charlie knew John quite well, as they had worked on several other criminal prosecutions in the past.

He also knew John's lovely wife, LeAnn, and their two wonderful kids, Lindsay and Zach, who are both grown up now and attending UCI (University of Irvine, California) and who will both perhaps be future Attorneys, District Attorneys, Mayors or Governors some day.

LeAnn is a legal assistant, soon to be an Attorney and also a very accomplished singer. She has one of the best voices that Charlie ever heard, she truly does. Charlie does not see them as much as he would like, but, he still considers them to be two of the best and most loyal personal friends that he has ever had in his entire life. He really does.

Charlie decided to take this very interesting and challenging case and agreed to accept $1,000.00 per diem (per day), plus all expenses. The confidential employment contract with the City of Anaheim would run for one month and it could be extended for another 30 days, depending upon the progress that he was making toward identifying and having the Heinous suspect arrested.

The first thing that good old Charlie did right after he accepted this assignment, he sent copies of the threatening emails and letters to his good friend Howard Wallace, the Director of the CIA (Central Intelligence Agency), in Langley, Virginia.

He first had called Howard on his private encrypted satellite cell phone and asked for his assistance with Charlie's newest case, which involved the Mayor of Anaheim, California. Howard as usual, immediately said, "Charlie my old buddy, anything you need, I am here for you."

Howard also told him that he had a close personal friend (Harry Callahan) at the FBI (Federal Bureau of Investigation or as some like to call it the, Federal Bureau of 'Intimidation'). And that he would forward the threatening emails and letters to him and have them compared to the many samples on file in the quite large FBI criminal threat Data Base.

Howard added that the specialists at the FBI should be able to tell us what email address the threats were actually sent from and also who sent them, if at all possible. The emails were signed by 'Dark Moon Rising', and the phony email address was somewhere in *Pyongyang*, the Capital of *North Korea*.

In the meantime, while his friend Howard was working on the very ominous emails/letters, Charlie took the unopened packages to his old buddy, Jim Bowen at the LAPD (Los Angeles Police Department), he was the Deputy Police Chief as well as the Watch Commander for most of Downtown LA (Los Angeles).

Jim had his Bomb Disposal unit open the suspicious packages in their Secure Bunker located by the LA Coliseum, just off of the 110 (Harbor Freeway) at the 10 (Santa Monica Freeway), right downtown LA.

The three parcels all had small but very powerful IED's (i.e., Improvised Explosive Devices), that could have easily killed Bumpy, or anyone whom opened the packages for him, such as a secretary or office staff member.

Bowen let Charlie watch from behind the bomb-proof barrier as his special team disarmed the three deadly devices. The team saved the bomb parts to compare to any similar ones that they had on file and also for future examination if they should get other IED's like these.

Jim told Charlie that he would let him know if they found anything out ASAP (as soon as possible). Bowen and Charlie go way, way back to the good (or bad) old days when they were both First Grade Detectives at the Infamous "Rampart Division" of the LAPD.

It was located right by Mac Arthur Park at Third and Alvarado streets. They had some bad apples (cops) at that particular police division however Charlie and Jim were two of the Good Guys. They truly were.

Bowen was a big man, 6'4", about 225, strong, muscular, not fat, a great talker and everybody liked him, even the people he arrested. Charlie never knew anyone who did not love to talk to Jim about Sports. You name the sport and he could tell you all about it and even the players.

He had the best sense of humor of any man Charlie ever worked with, he really did. He was also very Street Smart and intelligent, he went to Cal State University LA when he was young.

Also, he played a lot of football there and as a kid going up in big Bassett, (close to La Puente, San Gabriel Valley) California. He is married to a lovely, smart and very successful career woman (Roz). They live in a nice private community in Irvine, California.

Mr. Bernard Parks, who is very well-respected and very successful at helping out the citizens and public of LA for years and recently retired LA City Council Member, was the Chief of Police back in the Day. He was Fearless about going anywhere and at anytime Day or Night, in the City of LA. Mr. Parks, was quite intelligent, very hardworking, almost never slept, always on the job, and was extremely loyal to the men and woman who served with him.

He was also one of the Best Police Chiefs that the good City of LA has ever had, he really was.

To solve this quite serious criminal case, Charlie decided to start at square one. He looked deeply into Bumpy's background from childhood to the present day. And he did it real deeply. And, you know Charlie.

He is a very, very thorough man. He had a 'gut feeling' (the kind of intuition that he had developed over the 20 years as a LAPD Police Detective), that the perp was probably either a disgruntled former Real Estate customer or an ex-girlfriend/lover who The Donald dumped in his past.

Charlie remembered that very old saying, "Hell hath no fury like that of a woman scorned." He had seen many women like that in his Police and PI line of work however he saw the same thing with men as well.

When Charlie checked into the legal Records at the Santa Ana Court House, on Fourth Street he found that Bumpy had 121 prior and/or current Law Suits. Lots of them were Small Claims Suits (under $5,000.00) and not that serious really. Several, however, were for much larger amounts, much larger.

One was for One Million Dollars and several were for $250,000.00 to $500,000.00. And in all of these larger law suits, the people suing accused Bumpy of a Breach of "Good Faith and Fair Dealing" and/or some other illegal representation during a real estate transaction in the OC. Most of them involved houses, but, several were on Commercial and Industrial properties.

There were about 25 of these legal Claimants, out of the 121, that sounded to Charlie like they should be 'persons of interest' in this said case. All of these people had threatened Bumpy's Life or Limbs in the recent past. About 10 of the 25 had mentioned something about Blowing him to Kingdom come.

And, they all said that the Donald had ruined their health, finances, or lives in one way or another. Very interesting Charlie said to himself, very interesting indeed.

Charlie felt that the Second most likely group of candidates of this crime, were Bumpy's old 'Flames.' He considered himself, 'a man about town' so to speak and also very 'suave and debonair', as well as much more intelligent that most other people.

And he apparently had always felt that way about himself from what Charlie had heard from many, many people. Mr. Bump had been married three times before, for terms of 15, 5 and 3 years, respectively.

All of the Donald's three former wives as well as about five of his ex-girlfriends had documented hateful and vicious written and verbal threats, on file with the Anaheim Police Department. Charlie obtained copies of them over the internet.

Charlie decided to investigate 10 out of the 25 quite upset and emotionally as well as financially hurting Real Estate patrons first. After his initial investigation, he did not see the other 15 as viable suspects.

If he did not discover the identity of the person making the Threats, then he would move on forward and check out the 'love Interests' in Bumpy's life.

Charlie made up a list of those Top Ten people whom had been defrauded and had their lives ruined by the Donald. The list is presented Herewith:

SUSPECT NUMBER ONE

Susan 'Suzie' Brown - She was a 39-year-old single mom who was a software manager in Irvine. She bought a nice home in Newport Beach that turned out to be completely Termite infested. Bumpy promised her would pay the heavy pest control costs, but he never did. The Clear Termite Report he presented to close Escrow was later discovered to be a forgery.

SUSPECT NUMBER TWO

Roger Anthony 'Tony' Reese was a married 59-year-old Insurance Executive for State Farm Insurance in Brea (North Orange County). He bought a very nice home in the exclusive North Hills area of Brea. It turned out that the custom-built home was built on the site of an old oil well.

And, due to that, there were dangerous chemicals (cancer-causing possibly) in the soil and even some in his house. The Donald had hired a geologist to say that the toxins had all been removed.

SUSPECT NUMBER THREE

Homer James 'Jimmy' Williams was a 69-year-old retired Bank Executive from Wells Fargo Bank (the fifth largest bank in the USA), in downtown LA. He bought a 4-plex rental unit in Santa Ana. That property turned out to be in an 'eminent domain' area right next to the 5 Freeway.

So right after the Escrow closed, the City of Santa Ana, took control of the rental to widen the Freeway and paid Jimmy only $500,000.00 just after he paid the Bumpster One Million for it.

SUSPECT NUMBER FOUR

Sandra 'Sandi' Jones was a 49-year-old married woman and the owner of a very popular Bakery in the city of Orange. She bought the commercial building that housed her shop for $750,000.00. Mr. Bump provided her with a counterfeit Appraisal for One Million dollar, when in actuality the property was only worth around $500,000.00.

SUSPECT NUMBER FIVE

Sharon 'Shari' Samuel was a 35-year-old divorced mother of two neat kids and was a Sales manager at the Millennium BMW dealership at the auto center in Laguna Hills, located right off of the 405 Freeway.

She was very attractive and was very successful at selling high end vehicles like BMW's. She bought a cute little bungalow right on the water, in Laguna Beach for One Million dollars.

The home collapsed right after she moved into it due to age and salt water damage over the years. She is suing the Donald so that she may purchase another nice little home in Laguna.

SUSPECT NUMBER SIX

Alice 'Chris' Roundstone was a 29-year-old Flight Attendant for US Airways who flew out of the famous John Wayne Airport in the OC. She was a quite lovely blonde who was a part time actress. She had met Bumpy on a flight to Chicago and had dated him, on and off, for a few years.

The home she had bought from him in Corona del Mar was infested with cockroaches. They were so repulsive, she had to move out and sell the home at a loss of $350,000.00. Mr. Bump had promised her that he would reimburse her, but as in his usual manner, he never did.

SUSPECT NUMBER SEVEN

John 'Jack' Arredondo was the Chief Finance Manger for the city of Sunset Beach. He bought a nice but small ocean front home for $1 1/2 Million in lovely Seal Beach, the city right next door to Sunset. It turned out that the parking space in front of his home actually belonged to the neighbor.

And his space was way up the block, very inconvenient to say the least. Jack was suing Bumpy for $100,000.00 and fraud.

SUSPECT NUMBER EIGHT

Lawrence 'Larry' Nixon was a Professor at UCI (University of California at Irvine). He had purchased an older and small yet lovely home right on Balboa Island in Newport Beach. The Donald had told him that Boat Slip came with the home, but it did not. He was suing for $150,000.00. That was the going value for a Boat Dock on the Island.

SUSPECT NUMBER NINE

Elmer Thomas 'Tom' Cruise, was the General Manager of the famous *Honda Center* in Anaheim, where the Ducks Ice Hockey team plays. It is also right across the 57 (the OC Freeway) from the *Big A* (Anaheim Baseball Stadium) where the Angels play. They also have great Music Concerts there as well as the games. Charlie has been to several of them.

He saw, The Doobie Brothers (most of the audience was high), the incomparable Tony Bennett (Frank Sinatra's favorite vocalist), the still lovely and quite talented Stevie Nicks (Fleetwood Mac band-Charlie's favorite rock band), the still very young-looking Kenny Loggins ("Your mama doesn't dance, and your daddy don't rock n' roll)."

Which he sang with Jim Messina (Loggins and Messina were quite successful) as well as Chicago (the rock band legend and one of the most popular bands of all time).

Tom bought a lovely condo right on the Pacific Ocean in beautiful Ensenada, Baja California (i.e., Mexico). Once again, the only problem was that Bumpy did not hold the title to the property, it belonged to the local county government.

Tom paid $300,000.00 for the Hermosa (beautiful in Spanish) unit and lost every penny. You cannot file law suits there unless you are a Mexican citizen. Charlie really loves Ensenada and has vacationed there several times. He also loves the Mexican people who live there. They always treated him like a King, they truly did.

SUSPECT NUMBER TEN

Laurie 'Kathy' Turner was a Finance and Employee Benefits Supervisor at the old and very well -respected private college, Chapman University in the city of Orange. The Bumpster had sold her a cute little triplex on the marvelous Circle in that town. The only problem was that he did not have the real estate listing for that subject property, another Broker did.

Therefore, she did not get to buy the nice rental, she had planned to live in the largest unit and rent out the other two. She lost her $25,000.00, non-refundable deposit that she paid to Bumpy, which was a big part of her life savings.

Then, after making his suspect list and checking it twice (just like Santa Claus) and also doing a great deal of research of the Ten disgruntled former Real Estate customers with the assistance of John Anderson, the Orange County DA, and his great investigative staff.

Charlie's PI (Private Investigator) 'gut' (and LAPD ulcer) told him that either suspect number five, number six, or number seven, was most probably the 'guilty' party in this quite complicated investigation.

He sent a Security Activity Report of these three suspects to the city of Anaheim, the Anaheim PD, the OC DA, and Howard at the CIA. A copy of that said report is presented herein:

SUSPECT NUMBER FIVE

Sharon 'Shari' Samuel had a pending law suit against Mr. Bump, for One Million dollars. It was filed due to the fact that her 'cute as a button' little Bungalow in lovely Laguna Beach that she had bought from him collapsed right after she purchased it.

He had told her that it was insured for $1,500,000.00, but it turned out that the Insurance Policy he provided to close Escrow was Forged. She lost her whole down payment of $250,000.00, after which she had made Death Threats in writing to the Donald according to the Anaheim Police Department.

Also, she had reportedly told some of her BMW car dealership friends, that she would make Bumpy pay, "one way or another." The OC DA also found out that she was very knowledgeable about sending undocumented emails as well as having a good understanding of the whole internet.

And, her current macho boyfriend just got back from Kabul, Afghanistan, where he had been a Navy Seal. He was also considered an IED and bomb expert.

SUSPECT NUMBER SIX

Alice 'Chris' Roundstone also had a quite large law suit against Mr. Bump. She had dated him a few years ago for about two years, but she dumped him when she found out that he had two other girlfriends. One was an Actress in Hollywood. And, the other one was a model and did work for the Orange County GQ Magazine.

Also, the home that he had sold her was completely infested with roaches, ugh. It cost her $25,000.00 to get rid of them, not to even mention the mental stress of living with all of those 'unwanted' guests. He had stated to her that he would gladly reimburse her the money, but he never did, big surprise, right?

Charlie thought to himself, "Chris had two very good reasons to hate, and threaten Bumpy. He cheated on her, at least twice that we know of and he made her life miserable with those pests plus costing her a lot of money."

SUSPECT NUMBER SEVEN

John 'Jack' Arredondo, an expert with Finance and Computer Software. His law suit was due to the fact that the nice little Beach cottage, located in Seal Beach, did not even have a garage or car port. The garage Bumpy had pointed out actually belonged to the next-door neighbor.

Jack had to park up the street two blocks away, and it was not a locking garage, it was only a car port. The *Anaheim* Police discovered that Jack, had not only threatened the Donald, but several other individuals whom 'allegedly' did him wrong.

It was said that Jack, had the knowledge to send almost untraceable emails as well as hard-to-trace US Mail letters. The OC District Attorney also discovered that Jack had served in the US Marine Corps, in the Bomb Disposal Unit in Iraq back in 2005. That, told Charlie, he could have easily sent the emails/letters as well as the IED's in the mail.

Charlie now believed that out of the ten main Death Treat candidates, these three were the most likely parties against Donald 'Bumpy' Bump. Also, Charlie said to himself, "Suspect number Five (Sharon 'Shari' Samuel), might, just might, be the guilty party."

Then he thought, however, if it is not Shari, then Jack and Chris should be looked at as very viable suspects. And, as of this time, neither of them should be dismissed as possible perps, at least not yet, anyway.

Charlie planned on investigating Bumpy's jilted girlfriends now that he had gone through the potential real estate-related customers' list. He had some *loose ends* on a few old cases and some large expense claims to file. As Charlie always says - "Money talks and criminals walk, but not always." Sometimes lady justice does prevail.

FIVE

CHARLIE ABSOLUTELY LOVES 'The Beach Boys', the original California music style surfer band. As a kid he surfed the Huntington Beach State Pier in Surf City USA (Huntington Beach, California) with his old school wood surf boards. He when to the internet to remises about the good ole days.

When he was young, indestructible, fearless, strong, never sick, tall, dark and handsome. Well, Charlie said to himself, "Charlie at least you are still tall. One out of three at your age is not that back." Herein is what he gleamed from the internet:

The Beach Boys are an American rock band that were formed in Hawthorne, California in 1961. The group's original lineup consisted of brothers Brian, Dennis and Carl Wilson, their cousin Mike Love, and their friend Al Jardine. Emerging at the vanguard of the "California Sound", the band's early music gained international popularity for distinct vocal harmonies and lyrics that evoked a southern California youth culture of surfing, cars, and romance.

Influenced by jazz-based vocal groups, 1950s rock and roll, and doo-wop, Brian led the band to experiment with several genres ranging from pop ballads to psychedelic and baroque, while devising novel approaches to music production and arranging. While initially managed by the Wilsons' father Murry, Brian's creative ambitions and sophisticated songwriting abilities dominated the group's musical direction.

Released in 1966, the *Pet Sounds* album and the "Good Vibrations" single featured an intricate and multi-layered sound that represented a departure from the simple surf rock of the Beach Boys' early years. Soon after the dissolution of *Smile*, Brian gradually ceded control to the rest of the band, reducing his input due to mental health and substance abuse issues.

Dennis drowned in 1983 and Carl died of lung cancer in 1998. After Carl's death, many live configurations of the band fronted by Mike Love and Bruce Johnston continued to tour into the 2000s while other members pursued solo projects. For the band's 50th anniversary, the surviving co-founders briefly reunited for a new studio album and world tour.

The Beach Boys are one of the most critically acclaimed, commercially successful, and widely influential bands of all time, and are often touted as "America's Band", while AllMusic stated that their "unerring ability... made them America's first, best rock band." The group had over eighty songs chart worldwide, thirty-six of them US Top 40 hits (the most by an American rock band), four reaching number-one on the *Billboard* Hot 100 chart.

The Beach Boys have sold in excess of 100 million records worldwide, making them one of the world's best-selling bands of all time and are listed at number 12 on *Rolling Stone* magazine's 2004 list of the "100 Greatest Artists of All Time". They have received one Grammy Award for *The Smile Sessions* (2011). The core quintet of the three Wilsons, Love and Jardine were inducted into the Rock and Roll Hall of Fame in 1988.

HALL OF FAME

Members (1988):	Brian Wilson, Mike Love, Al Jardine, David Marks and Bruce Johnston
Past Band Members:	Dennis Wilson, Carl Wilson, Ricky Fataar and Blondie Chaplin

At the time of his sixteenth birthday on June 20, 1958, Brian Wilson shared a bedroom with his brothers, Dennis and Carl – aged thirteen and eleven, respectively – in their family home in Hawthorne. He had watched his father, Murry Wilson, play piano, and had listened intently to the harmonies of vocal groups such as the Four Freshmen. After dissecting songs such as "Ivory Tower" and "Good News", Brian would teach family members how to sing the background harmonies.

For his birthday that year, Brian received a reel-to-reel tape recorder. He learned how to overdub, using his vocals and those of Carl and their mother. Brian played piano with Carl and David Marks, an eleven-year-old long-time neighbor, playing guitars they had each received as Christmas presents.

Soon Brian and Carl were avidly listening to Johnny Otis' KFOX radio show. Inspired by the simple structure and vocals of the rhythm and blues songs he heard, Brian changed his piano-playing style and started writing songs. His enthusiasm interfered with his music studies at school. Family gatherings brought the Wilsons in contact with cousin Mike Love.

Brian taught Love's sister Maureen and a friend harmony. Later, Brian, Mike Love and two friends performed at Hawthorne High School. Brian also knew Al Jardine, a high school classmate who had already played guitar in a folk group called the Islanders.

Brian suggested to Jardine that they team up with his cousin and brother Carl. At these sessions, held in Brian's bedroom, "the Beach Boys sound" began to form. Love encouraged Brian to write songs, and gave the fledgling band its name: "The Pendletones", a portmanteau of "Pendleton", a style of woolen shirt popular at the time and "tone", the musical term.

Though surfing motifs were prominent in their early songs, Dennis was the only avid surfer in the group. He suggested that the group compose songs that celebrated the sport and the lifestyle that had developed around it within Southern California.

Jardine and a singer friend, Gary Winfrey, went to Brian to see if he could help out with a version of a folk song they wanted to record—"Sloop John B". In Brian's absence, the two spoke with their father, a music industry veteran of modest success.

Murry arranged for the Pendletones to meet his publisher, Hite Morgan. The group performed a slower ballad, "Their Hearts Were Full of Spring", but failed to impress Morgan. After an awkward pause, Dennis mentioned they had an original song, "Surfin'". Brian finished the song, and together with Mike Love, wrote "Surfin' Safari". The group rented guitars, drums, amplifiers and microphones, and practiced for three days while the Wilsons' parents were on a short vacation.

In October 1961, the Pendletones recorded the two surfing song demos in twelve takes at Keen Recording Studio. Murry brought the demos to Herb Newman, owner of Candix Records and Era Records, and he signed the group on December 8, 1961. When the boys eagerly unpacked the first box of singles – released both under the Candix label, and also as a promo issue under X Records (Morgan's label) – they were shocked to see their band had been renamed as the Beach Boys.

Murry Wilson called Morgan and learned that Candix wanted to name the group the Surfers to directly associate them with the increasingly popular teen sport. But Russ Regan, a young promoter with Era Records – who later became president of 20th Century Fox Records – noted that there already existed a group by that name, and he suggested calling them the Beach Boys.

Released in December 1961, "Surfin'" soon aired on KFWB and KRLA, two of Los Angeles' most influential teen radio stations. It was a hit on the West Coast, going to number three in Southern California, and peaked at number 75 on the national pop charts. By the final weeks of 1961 "Surfin'" had sold more than 40,000 copies.

Though Murry effectively seized managerial control of the band, Brian acknowledged that he "...deserves credit for getting us off the ground... he hounded us mercilessly... [but] also worked hard himself." In the first half of February 1962, Jardine left the band and was replaced by Marks.

The band recorded two more originals on April 19 at Western Studios, Los Angeles: "Lonely Sea" and "409". They also re-recorded "Surfin' Safari". On June 4, the band released their second single "Surfin' Safari" backed with "409".

At the beginning of a tour of the Mid-West in April 1963, Jardine rejoined the Beach Boys at Brian's request. As he began playing live gigs again, Brian left the road to focus on writing and recording. The result of this arrangement produced the albums *Surfer Girl*, released on September 16, 1963 and *Little Deuce Coupe*, released less than a month later on October 7, 1963.

Around this time, Brian began using members of the Wrecking Crew to augment his increasingly demanding studio arrangements. The band released a standalone Christmas-themed single, "Little Saint Nick", in December 1963, backed with an a capella rendition of the scriptural song "The Lord's Prayer". The A-side peaked at number 3 on the US Billboard Christmas chart.

In June 1964, Brian began recording the bulk of The Beach Boys' Christmas Album with a forty-one-piece studio orchestra in collaboration with Four Freshmen arranger Dick Reynolds. Released in December, it was divided between five new, original Christmas-themed songs, and seven reinterpretations of traditional Christmas songs.

One single from the album, "The Man with All the Toys", was released, peaking at number 6 on the US Billboard Christmas chart. On October 29, the Beach Boys performed for *The T.A.M.I. Show*, a concert film intended to bring together a wide range of hit-making musicians for a one-off performance. The result was released to movie theaters one month later.

By the end of the year, the stress of road travel, composing, producing and maintaining a high level of creativity became too much for Brian. On December 23, while on a flight from Los Angeles to Houston, he suffered a panic attack only hours after performing with the Beach Boys on the musical variety series *Shindig!*.

In January 1965, he announced his withdrawal from touring to concentrate entirely on songwriting and record production. For the rest of 1964 and into 1965, Glen Campbell served as Wilson's temporary replacement in concert, until his own career success pulled him from the group in April 1965.

Bruce Johnston was asked to locate a replacement for Campbell; having failed to find one, Johnston himself became a full-time member of the band on May 19, 1965, first replacing Brian on the road and later contributing in the studio, beginning with the vocal sessions for "California Girls" on June 4, 1965.

After Brian stopped touring in 1965, he became a full-time studio artist, showcasing a great leap forward with *The Beach Boys Today!*, an album containing a suite-like structure divided by songs and ballads, and portended the Album Era with its cohesive artistic statement. During the recording sessions for *Today!*

Love told Melody Maker that he and the band wanted to look beyond surf rock and to avoid living in the past or resting on their laurels. The resulting LP had largely guitar-oriented pop songs such as "Dance, Dance, Dance" and "Good to My Baby" on side A with B-side ballads such as "Please Let Me Wonder" and "She Knows Me Too Well".

In June 1965, the band released Summer Days (And Summer Nights!!). The album included a reworked arrangement of "Help Me, Rhonda" which became the band's second number one single in the spring of 1965, displacing the Beatles' "Ticket to Ride". "Let Him Run Wild" tapped into the youthful angst that later pervaded their music. In November 1965, the group followed their US number-three-charting "California Girls" from *Summer Days (And Summer Nights!!)* with another top-twenty single, "The Little Girl I Once Knew".

It was considered the band's most experimental statement thus far, using silence as a pre-chorus, clashing keyboards, moody brass and vocal tics. The single continued Brian's ambitions for daring arrangements, featuring unexpected tempo changes and numerous false endings. Perhaps too extreme an arrangement to go much higher than its number 20 peak, it was the band's second single not to reach the top ten since their 1962 breakthrough.

Capitol demanded a Beach Boys LP for the 1965 Christmas season, and to appease them, Brian conceived *Beach Boys' Party!*, a live-in-the-studio album consisting mostly of acoustic covers of 1950s rock and R&B songs, in addition to covers of three Beatles songs, Bob Dylan's "The Times They Are a-Changin'", and idiosyncratic re-recordings of the group's earlier hits.

In December they scored an unexpected number two hit (number three in the UK) with "Barbara Ann", which Capitol released as a single with no band input. Originally by the Regents, it became one of the Beach Boys' most recognized hits.

Pet Sounds is regarded as one of the greatest albums of all time and is one of the most universally acclaimed in rock *history*

In 1966, the Beach Boys formally established their use of unconventional instruments and elaborate layers of vocal harmonies on their groundbreaking record *Pet Sounds*. It is considered Brian's most concise demonstration of his production and songwriting expertise. With songs such as "Wouldn't It Be Nice" and "Sloop John B", the album's innovative sounds cape incorporates elements of pop, jazz, classical, exotica, and the avant-garde.

The instrumentation combines found sounds such as bicycle bells and dog whistles with classically inspired orchestrations and the usual rock set-up of drums and guitars; among others, silverware, accordions, plucked piano strings, barking dogs, and plastic water jugs. For the basic rhythmic feel for "God Only Knows", harpsichord, piano with slap back echo, sleigh bells, and strings spilled into each other to create a rich blanket of sound.

Released in May, *Pet Sounds* eventually peaked at number eleven in the US and number two in the UK. This helped the Beach Boys become the strongest selling album act in the UK for the final quarter of 1966, dethroning the three-year reign of native bands such as the Beatles. Met with a lukewarm critical reception in the US, *Pet Sounds* was indifferently promoted by Capitol and failed to become the major hit Wilson had hoped it would be.

In a 1972 review of *Pet Sounds*, music journalist Stephen Davis wrote.

Pet Sounds went on to be acknowledged as an important historical and cultural work, remaining today as an evocative release with distinctive lushness and melancholy. Beyond pop and rock, *Pet Sounds* expanded the field of music production. It was massively influential upon its release, vaunting the band to the top level of rock innovators.

It is one of the earliest rock concept albums, one of the earliest concept albums of the counterculture era, and an early album in the emerging psychedelic rock style, signaling a turning point wherein rock, which previously had been considered dance music, became music that was made for listening to.

Sir Paul McCartney named it one of his favorite albums of all time on multiple occasions, calling it the primary impetus for the Beatles' album

Sgt. Pepper's Lonely Hearts Club Band (1967). In 2003, *Pet Sounds* was ranked second in "The 500 Greatest Albums of All Time" list selected by *Rolling Stone*, behind only *Sgt. Pepper*.

"Good Vibrations" and *Smile*. Seeking to expand on *Pet Sounds'* advances, Wilson began an even more ambitious project: "Good Vibrations". Like *Pet Sounds*, Brian opted for an eclectic array of instruments rarely heard in pop music. Described by Brian as a "pocket symphony", it contains a mixture of classical, rock, and exotic instruments structured around a cut-up mosaic of musical sections represented by several discordant key and modal shifts. It became the Beach Boys' biggest hit to date, [and a US and UK number one single in 1966.

The single was an unequivocal milestone in studio productions and continued in establishing Brian as an extender of popular tastes. To the counterculture of the 1960s, "Good Vibrations" served as an anthem.

The group established a short-lived film production company, called Home Movies, during this time. It was supposed to have created live action film and television properties starring the Beach Boys. However, the company completed only one music video, for "Good Vibrations", though various other psychedelic sequences and segments exist.

I'm doing the spiritual sound, a white spiritual sound. Religious music...That's the whole movement...That's where I'm going and it's going to scare a lot of people when I get there.

—Brian Wilson quoted in *Goodbye Surfing, Hello God!* (1967), by Jules Siegel.

Smile would go on to become the most legendary unreleased album in the history of popular music. In the decades following its non-release, it became the subject of intense speculation and mystique. Many believe that, had the album been released, it would have substantially altered the group's direction and established them at the vanguard of rock innovators.

Many factors combined to put intense pressure on Brian Wilson as *Smile* neared completion: his mental instability, the pressure to create despite fierce internal opposition to his new music, the relatively unenthusiastic response to *Pet Sounds* in the United States, Carl Wilson's draft resistance, and a major dispute with Capitol Records. Furthermore, Wilson's reliance on both prescription drugs and amphetamines exacerbated his underlying mental health problems.

Comparable to Brian Jones and Syd Barrett, Brian Wilson's use of psychedelic drugs—especially LSD—led to a nervous breakdown in the late-1960s. As his legend grew, the *Smile* period came to be seen as the pivotal episode in his decline, and he became tagged as one of the most notorious celebrity drug casualties of the rock era.

SIX

CHARLIE DISCOVERED SOME additional previously unknown as well as very interesting personal information on his all time Favorite Band the Fabulous Beach Boys. One item he read about was the 'Smile' Album (1967) came out on national radio stations at about the same time as the mental decline of the great Brian Wilson. At this time Wilson was 'tagged' as one of the most notorious celebrity drug casualty of the whole Rock n' Roll era (up until that time).

Marijuana, all kinds of psychedelic drugs, especially LSD, led to a severe emotional breakdown in the late 1960's of Wilson. The wild Honey album was released three months later and was much better recognized and respected by fans and musical critics. By 1967 the surfer music pioneers the Beach boys, were said to have become Cultural Dinosaurs.

Also thank God Brian Wilson would make a total recovery from his serious and quite deep depression and excessive drug use. He is still touring with some old members of the Band and doing some TV interviews with his new wife. She is credited with saving his life and getting him back with us music lovers.

Some *Smile* tracks were salvaged and re-recorded in scaled-down versions at Brian's new home studio. Along with the single version of "Good Vibrations", these tracks were released on the album *Smiley Smile*, which elicited positive critical and commercial response abroad.

"[By] 1967, the Beach Boys had become cultural dinosaurs. And it happened almost overnight....Monterey was a gathering place for the 'far out' sounds of the 'new' rock, and the Beach Boys in concert really had no exotic sounds to display. The net result of all [their] internal and external turmoil was that the Beach Boys didn't go...and it is thought that this non-appearance was what really turned the 'underground' tide against them."
—David Leaf

Compounding the group's recent setbacks, their public image took a cataclysmic hit following their withdrawal from the 1967 Monterey Pop Festival for the reason that they had no new material to play while their forthcoming single and album lay in limbo. Their cancellation was seen as "...a damning admission that they were washed up [and] unable to compete with the new music."

This notion was exacerbated by *Rolling Stone* writer Jann Wenner, who in contemporary publications criticized Brian Wilson for his oft-repeated "genius" label, which he called a "promotional shuck" and an attempt to compare him with the Beatles.

However, Wenner later responded to their *Wild Honey* album with more optimism, remarking two months later that "[i]n any case it's good to see that the Beach Boys are getting their heads straight once again".

While being interviewed in August 1967 for the failed live album *Lei'd in Hawaii*, Brian admitted: "I think rock n' roll–the pop scene–is happening. It's great. But I think basically, the Beach Boys are squares. We're not happening."

Former band publicist Derek Taylor later recalled a conversation with Brian and Dennis where they denied that the group had ever written surf music or songs about cars, and that the Beach Boys had never been involved with the surf and hot rod fads, as Taylor claimed, "...they would not concede."

In spring 1968, Dennis began a strained relationship with musician Charles Manson, which persisted for several months afterward. Dennis bought him time at Brian's home studio where recording sessions were attempted while Brian stayed in his room. Dennis then proposed that Manson be signed to Brother Records.

Brian reportedly disliked Charlie, and so a deal was never made. Without Manson's involvement, the Beach Boys did record one song penned by Manson: "Cease to Exist", rewritten as "Never Learn Not To Love".

The idea of the Beach Boys recording one of his songs reportedly thrilled Manson, and it was released as a Beach Boys single. After accruing a large monetary debt to the group, Dennis deliberately omitted Manson's credit on its release while also altering the song's arrangement and lyrics.

This greatly angered Manson. Growing fearful, Dennis gradually distanced himself from *Manson*, whose family had taken over his home. He was eventually convicted for murder conspiracy; from there on, Dennis was too afraid of the Manson family to ever speak publicly on his relationship, let alone testify against him.

On April 12, 1969, the band revisited their 1967 lawsuit against Capitol Records after they alleged an audit undertaken revealed the band were owed over US$2,000,000 (US$12,860,000 today) for unpaid royalties and production duties. The band's contract with Capitol Records expired on June 30, 1969, after which Capitol Records deleted the Beach Boys' catalog from print, effectively cutting off their royalty flow.

In November 1969, Murry Wilson sold Sea of Tunes, the Beach Boys' catalog, to Irving Almo Music, a decision that, according to Marilyn Wilson, devastated Brian. In late 1969, the Beach Boys reactivated their Brother label and signed with Reprise. Around this time, the band commenced recording a new album. By the time the Beach Boys tenure ended with Capitol in 1969, they had sold 65 million records worldwide, closing the decade as the most commercially successful American group in popular music.

In 1970, armed with the new Reprise contract, the band appeared rejuvenated, releasing the album *Sunflower* to critical acclaim in the UK but indifference in the US. The album features a strong group presence with significant writing contributions from all band members.

Brian was active during this period, writing or co-writing seven of the twelve songs on *Sunflower* and performing at half of the band's domestic concerts in 1970. *Sunflower* reached number 29 in the UK and number 151 in the US, the band's lowest domestic chart showing to that point.

A version of "Cottonfields" arranged by Al Jardine appeared on European releases of *Sunflower* and as a single, reached number one in Australia, Norway, South Africa and Sweden and the top-five in six other countries, including the UK.

After *Sunflower*, the band hired Jack Rieley as their manager. Under Rieley's management, the group's music began emphasizing political and social awareness. During this time, Carl Wilson gradually assumed leadership of the band and Rieley contributed lyrics.

On August 30, 1971 the band released *Surf's Up*, named after the Brian Wilson/Van Dyke Parks composition "Surf's Up". The album was moderately successful, reaching the US top 30, a marked improvement over their recent releases.

While the record charted, the Beach Boys added to their renewed fame by performing a near-sellout set at *Carnegie Hall*, followed by an appearance with the Grateful Dead at Fillmore East on April 27, 1971.

The live shows during this era included reworked arrangements of many of the band's previous songs. A large portion of their set lists culled from *Pet Sounds* and *Smile*, as author Domenic Priore observes, "They basically played what they could have played at the Monterey Pop Festival in the summer of 1967."

Johnston ended his first stint with the band shortly after *Surf's Up*'s release, reportedly because of friction with Rieley. At Carl's suggestion, the addition of Ricky Fataar and Blondie Chaplin in February 1972 led to a dramatic restructuring in the band's sound. The album *Carl and the Passions – "So Tough"* was an uncharacteristic mix that included two songs written by Fataar and Chaplin.

For their next project the band, their families, assorted associates and technicians moved to the Netherlands for the summer of 1972. They rented a farmhouse to convert into a makeshift studio where recording sessions for the new project would take place. By the end of their sessions, the band felt they had produced one of their strongest efforts yet. Reprise, however, felt that the album required a strong single.

This resulted in the song "Sail On, Sailor", a collaboration between Brian Wilson, Tandyn Almer, Ray Kennedy, Jack Rieley and Van Dyke Parks featuring a soulful lead vocal by Chaplin. Reprise subsequently approved and the resulting album, *Holland*, was released early in 1973, peaking at number 37.

Brian's musical children story, *Mount Vernon and Fairway (A Fairy Tale)*, narrated by Rieley and strongly influenced by Randy Newman's *Sail Away* (1972), was included as a bonus EP. Despite indifference from Reprise, the band's concert audience started to grow.

The Beach Boys in Concert, a double album documenting the 1972 and 1973 US tours, was another top-30 album and became the band's first gold record under Reprise. During this period the band established itself as one of America's most popular live acts.

Chaplin and Fataar helped organize the concerts to obtain a high -quality live performance, playing material off *Surf's Up*, *Carl and the Passions* and *Holland* and adding songs from their older catalog. This concert arrangement lifted them back into American public prominence. In late 1973, the 41-song soundtrack to *American Graffiti* was released including the band's early songs "Surfin' Safari" and "All Summer Long".

The album was a catalyst in creating a wave of nostalgia that reintroduced the Beach Boys into contemporary American consciousness. In 1974, Capitol Records issued *Endless Summer*, the band's first major pre-*Pet Sounds* greatest hits package. The compilation surged to the top of the *Billboard* album charts and was the group's first multi-million selling record since "Good Vibrations". It remained on the charts for two years.

Capitol followed with a second compilation, *Spirit of America*, which also sold well. With these compilations, the Beach Boys became one of the most popular acts in rock, propelling themselves from opening for Crosby, Stills,

Nash and Young to headliners selling out basketball arenas in a matter of weeks. *Rolling Stone* named the Beach Boys the "Band of the Year" for 1974, solely on the basis of their juggernaut touring schedule and material written over a decade earlier.

Rieley, who remained in the Netherlands after *Holland*'s release, was relieved of his managerial duties in late 1973. Chaplin also left in late 1973 after an argument with Steve Love, the band's business manager (and Mike's brother). Fataar remained until 1974, when he was offered a chance to join a new group led by future Eagles member Joe Walsh. Chaplin's replacement, James William Guercio, started offering the group career advice that resulted in his becoming their new manager.

Under Guercio, the Beach Boys staged a highly successful 1975 joint concert tour with Chicago, with each group performing some of the other's songs, including their previous year's collaboration on Chicago's hit "Wishing You Were Here". Beach Boys vocals were also heard on *Elton John*'s 1974 hit "Don't Let the Sun Go Down on Me".

Nostalgia had settled into the Beach Boys' hype; the group had not officially released any new material since 1973's *Holland*. While their concerts continuously sold out, the stage act slowly changed from a contemporary presentation followed by oldies encores to an entire show made up of mostly pre-1967 music.

Recorded in the wake of California Music's demise, a super group that would have involved Brian Wilson, Bruce Johnston, and record producer Terry Melcher, *15 Big Ones* (1976) marked Brian's return as a major force in the group.

The album included new songs by Brian, as well as cover versions of oldies such as "Rock and Roll Music", "Blueberry Hill", and "In the Still of the Night". "Rock and Roll Music" peaked at number 5 in the US. Brian and Love's "It's O.K." was in the vein of their early sixties style, and was a moderate hit.

The album was publicized by an August 1976 NBC-TV special, simply titled *The Beach Boys*. The special, produced by *Saturday Night Live* (SNL) creator Lorne Michaels, featured appearances by *SNL* cast members John Belushi and Dan Aykroyd.

For the remainder of 1976 to early 1977, Brian spent his time making sporadic public appearances and producing the band's next album *Love You* (1977), a quirky collection of 14 songs mostly written, arranged and produced by Brian. Brian revealed to Peter Ames Carlin that *Love You* is one of his favorite Beach Boys releases, telling him "That's when it all happened for me. That's where my heart lies." *Love You* peaked at number 28 in the UK and number 53 in the US and developed a cult following; regarded as one of the band's best albums by fans and critics alike, and an early work of synthpop.

"A diseased bunch of losers if ever there was one ... But the miracle is that the Beach Boys have made that disease sound like the literal baby flesh pink of health ... Maybe it's just that unprickable and ingenuous wholesomeness that accounts not only for their charm, but for their beauty—a beauty so awesome that listening to them at their best is like being in some vast dream cathedral decorated with a thousand gleaming American pop culture icons."
—Lester Bangs in a review of Love You for Circus, June 9, 1977

After *Love You* was released, Brian began to record and assemble *Adult/Child*, an unreleased effort largely consisting of songs written by Wilson from 1976 and 1977 with select big band arrangements by Dick Reynolds. Though publicized as the Beach Boys' next release, *Adult/Child* caused tension within the group and was ultimately shelved. Following this period, his concert appearances with the band gradually diminished and their performances were occasionally erratic.

The band broke up for two and a half weeks, until a meeting on September 17 at Brian's house. In light of a potential new Caribou Records contract the parties negotiated a settlement resulting in Love gaining control of Brian's vote in the group, allowing Love and Jardine to outvote Carl and Dennis Wilson on any matter.

Dennis withdrew from the group to focus on his second solo album entitled *Bambu*. The album was shelved just as alcoholism and marital problems overcame all three Wilson brothers. Carl appeared intoxicated during concerts (especially at appearances for their 1978 Australia tour) and Brian gradually slid back into addiction and an unhealthy lifestyle.

After departing Reprise, the Beach Boys signed with CBS Records. They received a substantial advance and were paid $1 million per album even as CBS deemed their preliminary review of the band's first product, *L.A. (Light Album)* as unsatisfactory. Faced with the realization that Brian was unable to contribute, the band recruited Johnston as producer. The result paid off, as "Good Timin'" became a top 40 single.

The group enjoyed moderate success with a disco reworking of the *Wild Honey* song "Here Comes the Night", followed by their highest charting UK single in nine years: Jardine's "Lady Lynda" peaked at number 6 in the UK Singles Chart. The album was followed in 1980 by *Keepin' the Summer Alive*, with Johnston once again producing. Barring an appearance on percussion on the closing track, "Endless Harmony", Dennis was absent from this album.

In 1981, Carl quit the group due to unhappiness with the band's nostalgia format and lackluster live performances, subsequently pursuing a solo career. He returned in May 1982 – after approximately 14 months of being away—on the condition that the group reconsider their rehearsal and touring policies and refrain from "Las Vegas-type" engagements.

From 1980 through 1982, the Beach Boys and The Grass Roots performed Independence Day concerts at the National Mall in Washington, D.C., attracting large crowds. However, in April 1983, James G. Watt, President Ronald Reagan's Secretary of the Interior, banned Independence Day concerts on the Mall by such groups. Watt said that "rock bands" that had performed on the Mall on Independence Day in 1981 and 1982 had encouraged drug use and alcoholism and had attracted "the wrong element", who would steal from attendees.

During the ensuing uproar, which included over 40,000 complaints to the Department of the Interior, the Beach Boys stated that the Soviet Union, which had invited them to perform in Leningrad in 1978, "...obviously ... did not feel that the group attracted the wrong element." Vice President *George H. W. Bush* said of the Beach Boys, "They're my friends and I like their music".

Watt later apologized to the band after learning that President Reagan and First Lady *Nancy Reagan* were fans. White House staff presented Watt with a plaster foot with a hole in it, showing that he had "shot himself in the foot". The band returned to D.C. for Independence Day in 1984 and performed to a crowd of 750,000 people.

Founding drummer Dennis Wilson's alcoholism continued to escalate, and on December 28, 1983, he drowned in *Marina del Rey* while diving from a friend's boat trying to recover items he had previously thrown overboard in fits of rage. Despite his death, the Beach Boys continued as a successful touring act.

On July 4, 1985, the Beach Boys played to an afternoon crowd of one million in Philadelphia and the same evening they performed for over 750,000 people on the Mall in Washington. They also appeared nine days later at the *Live Aid* concert. That year, they released the eponymous album *The Beach Boys* and enjoyed a resurgence of interest later in the 1980s, assisted by tributes such as David Lee Roth's hit version of "California Girls".

"Getcha Back", released from the album, gave the group a number 26 single in the US. Following this, the group put out "Rock 'n' Roll to the Rescue" (US, number 68) and a cover of the Mamas & the Papas' "California Dreamin'" (US, number 57). In 1987, they played with the rap group The Fat Boys, performing the song "Wipe Out" and filming a music video. It was a number 12 single in the US. and a number two rank in the UK.

By 1988, Brian had drifted from the Beach Boys and released his first solo album, *Brian Wilson*, which received critical acclaim. During this period the band unexpectedly claimed their first US number one hit single in 22 years with "Kokomo", which had appeared in the movie *Cocktail*, and soon became the band's largest selling single of all time.

Inducted into the Rock and Roll Hall of Fame earlier in the year, the group became the second artist after Aretha Franklin to hit number one in the US after their induction. They released the album *Still Cruisin'*, which went gold in the US and gave them their best chart showing since 1976. In 1990, the band gathered several studio musicians and recorded the Melcher-produced title track.

A lawsuit was filed by Brian in 1989 to reclaim the rights to his songs and the group's publishing company, Sea of Tunes, which he had supposedly signed away to his father Murry in 1969. He successfully argued that he had not been mentally fit to make an informed decision and that his father had potentially forged his signature. While Wilson failed to regain his copyrights, he was awarded $25 million for unpaid royalties.

Soon after Wilson won his case, Love discovered that Murry Wilson had not properly credited him as co-writer on 79 Beach Boys songs. With Love and Brian unable to determine exactly what Love was properly owed, Love sued Brian in 1992, winning $13 million in 1994 for lost royalties. 35 of the group's songs were then amended to credit Love.

In 1993, the band appeared in Michael Feeney Callan's film *The Beach Boys Today*, which included in-depth interviews with all members except Brian. Carl confided to Callan that Brian would record again with the band at some point in the near future. A few Beach Boys sessions devoted to new Brian Wilson compositions occurred during the mid-1990s, but they remain largely unreleased, and the album was quickly aborted due to tenuous relations.

In February 1996, the Beach Boys guested with Status Quo on a re-recording of "Fun, Fun, Fun", which became a British Top-30 hit. In June, the group worked with comedian Jeff Foxworthy on the recording *Howdy from Maui*, and eventually released *Stars and Stripes Vol. 1* in August 1996.

The album consisted of country renditions of several Beach Boys hits, performed by popular country artists such as Toby Keith *and* Willie Nelson. Brian, who was in a better mental state at the time, acted as co-producer.

In early 1997, Carl was diagnosed with lung cancer and brain cancer after years of heavy smoking. Despite his terminal condition, Carl continued to perform with the band on its 1997 summer tour while undergoing chemotherapy. During performances, he sat on a stool and needed oxygen after every song. However, Carl was able to stand when he played on "God Only Knows". Carl died on February 6, 1998, two months after the death of the Wilsons' mother, Audree.

Following Carl's death, the remaining members splintered. Love, Johnston and former guitarist Marks continued to tour without Jardine, initially as "America's Band", but following several cancelled bookings under that name, they sought authorization through Brother Records Inc. (BRI) to tour as "The Beach Boys" and secured the necessary license.

In turn, Jardine began to tour regularly with his band dubbed "Beach

Boys: Family & Friends" until he ran into legal issues for using the name without license. Meanwhile, Jardine sued Love and Brian, claiming that he had been excluded from their concerts.

BRI, through its longtime attorney, Ed McPherson, sued Jardine in Federal Court. Jardine, in turn, counter-claimed against BRI for wrongful termination. BRI ultimately prevailed after several years. Mike Love was allowed to continue to tour as The Beach Boys, while Jardine was prohibited from touring using any form of the name.

Released from Landy's control, Brian Wilson sought different treatments for his illnesses that aided him in his solo career. He toured regularly with his backing band consisting of members of Wondermints and other LA/Chicago musicians. Marks also maintained a solo career. Their tours remained reliable draws, with Wilson and Jardine both remaining legal members of the Beach Boys organization and BRI.

The surviving group members appeared as themselves for the 1998 documentary film *Endless Harmony: The Beach Boys Story*, directed by Alan Boyd. Following the success of 1997's *The Pet Sounds Sessions*, many compilations were then issued by Capitol containing new archival material: *Endless Harmony Soundtrack* (1998), *Ultimate Christmas* (1998), and *Hawthorne, CA* (2001).

In 2004, Wilson recorded and released his solo album *Brian Wilson Presents Smile*, a reinterpretation of the *Smile* project that he initiated with the Beach Boys thirty-six years earlier. That September, Wilson issued a free CD through the *Mail On, Sunday* that included Beach Boys songs he'd recently rerecorded, five of which he'd co-authored with Love.

The 10-track compilation had 2.6 million copies distributed and prompted Love to file a lawsuit in November 2005; he claimed the promotion hurt the sales of the original recordings. Love's suit was dismissed in 2007 when a judge determined that there were no triable issues.

On June 13, 2006, the five surviving Beach Boys (Wilson, Love, Jardine, Johnston, and Marks) appeared together for the celebration of the 40th anniversary of *Pet Sounds* and the double-platinum certification of their greatest hits compilation, *Sounds of Summer: The Very Best of The Beach Boys*, in a ceremony atop the Capitol Records building in Hollywood. Plaques were awarded for their efforts, with Wilson accepting on behalf of Dennis and Carl.

On October 31, 2011, the Beach Boys released surviving 1960s recordings from *Smile* in the form of *The Smile Sessions*.

In February 2011, the Beach Boys released "Don't Fight the Sea", a charity single to aid the victims of the 2011 Japan earthquake. The single, released on Jardine's 2011 album *A Postcard from California* featured Jardine, Wilson, Love and Johnston, with prerecorded vocals by Carl Wilson. Rumors then circulated regarding a potential 50th anniversary band reunion.

On December 16, 2011, it was announced that Wilson, Love, Jardine, Johnston and Marks would reunite for a new album and 50th anniversary tour in 2012 to include a performance at the New Orleans Jazz Festival in April 2012. On February 12, 2012, the Beach Boys performed at the 2012 Grammy Awards, in what was billed as a "special performance" by organizers.

It marked the group's first live performance to include Brian since 1996. The Beach Boys then appeared at the April 10, 2012, season opener for the Los Angeles Dodgers and performed "Surfer Girl" and "The Star-Spangled Banner".

In April, the new album's title was revealed as *That's Why God Made the Radio*. The first single from the album, the title track, made its national radio debut April 25, 2012, on ESPN's *Mike and Mike in the Morning* and was released on iTunes and other digital platforms on April 26.

That's Why God Made the Radio debuted at number three on US charts, making US chart history by expanding the group's span of *Billboard* 200 top ten albums across 49 years and one week, passing the Beatles with 47 years of top ten albums.

Later in 2012, the group released the *Fifty Big Ones* and *Greatest Hits* compilations along with reissues of 12 of their albums. The next year, the group released *Live – The 50th Anniversary Tour* a 41 song, 2-CD set documenting their *50th Anniversary Tour*.

In June 2012, Love announced additional touring dates that would not feature Wilson. Wilson then denied knowledge of these new dates. On October 5, Love announced in a self-written press release to the *LA Times* that the band would return to its pre-50th Reunion Tour lineup with him and Johnston touring as the Beach Boys without Wilson, Jardine, and Marks:

I did not fire Brian Wilson from the Beach Boys. I cannot fire Brian Wilson from the Beach Boys ... I do not have such authority. And even if I did, I would never fire Brian Wilson from the Beach Boys. ... This tour was always envisioned as a limited run ...

As the year went on, Brian and Al wanted to keep the 50th anniversary tour going beyond the 75 dates ... However, ... we had already set up shows in smaller cities with ... the configuration that had been touring together every year for the last 13 years. Brian and Al would not be joining for these small market dates, as was long agreed upon.

Jardine, Marks, Johnston and Love appeared together at the 2014 Ella Awards Ceremony, where Love was honored for his work as a singer. Marks sang "409" in honor of Love, and Jardine performed "Help Me Rhonda". They closed the show with "Fun, Fun, Fun". Wilson's long-time band associate Jeff Foskett also appeared, but not Wilson. On May 15, 2014 the touring Beach Boys (Love and Johnston) announced a tour celebrating "50 Years of 'Fun Fun Fun'", named for their 1964 single.

The tour featured the addition of Foskett, who replaced Mike's son Christian. Foskett left Wilson's band due to encumbering responsibilities and hopes that Wilson and Love's band would someday converge, believing that the two Beach Boys don't "personally have a problem with each other."

As of September 2014, Jardine has maintained that a continued reunion with the Beach Boys is "really up to him [Love] ... He claims he didn't, that he fired us after the reunion ... He's a brilliant songwriter, and unfortunately, he has brilliant lawyers. We wish him all the best, but doggonit, you know, we'd like to be Beach Boys, too. There you go."

As Jardine restates "[Love] doesn't really want to work with us", biographer Jon Stebbins speculated that Love declined to continue working with the group due to the lesser control he had over the touring process, coupled with the lower financial gain, noting: "Night after night after night after night, Mike is making less money getting reminded that Brian is more popular than him. And he has to answer to people instead of calling all the shots himself."

In 2015, *Soundstage* aired an episode featuring Wilson performing with Jardine and former Beach Boys Blondie Chaplin and Ricky Fataar at The Venetian in Las Vegas. In April 2015, when asked if he was interested in making music with Love again, Wilson replied: "I don't think so, no," later adding in July that he "doesn't talk to the Beach Boys [or] Mike Love."

On July 25, 2015 Love said: "If you get Brian and I, we might go to the piano. But with every band there are cliques that are formed with management, wives, agents, publicists — and the tendency is with some people is they tend to lionize or make one person more important than the others. ... The Beach Boys and all these bands that ever existed are a team. I learned as captain of my cross-country team that you don't put a person down to get their best efforts, you encourage them."

SEVEN

CHARLIE FOUND THE last of the historical account of the Band, the indescribable and marvelously talented Beach Boys. They have been compared with many groups exceptionally talented bands over the years. Including the *Ventures*, the *Association*, the *Letterman*, among many, many other wonderful bands.

The *Original* Beach Boys band members were:
Brian Wilson (Brother), Dennis Wilson (Brother) – Deceased, Carl Wilson (Brother) – Deceased, Mike Love (Cousin), and
Al Jardine (Friend)

Band still currently touring as the 'Beach Boys':
Mike Love and David Marks

Also, still touring as the 'Surf Band':
Al Jardine and Blondie Chaplin and Ricky Fataar

In *Understanding Rock: Essays in Musical Analysis*, music theorist Daniel Harrison summarizes:

Even from their inception, the Beach Boys were an experimental group. They combined, as Jim Miller has put it, "the instrumental sleekness of the Ventures, the lyric sophistication of Chuck Berry, and the vocal expertise of some weird cross between the Lettermen and Frankie Lymon and the Teenagers" with lyrics who's images, idioms, and concerns were drawn from the rarefied world of the middle-class white male southern California teenager....

[But] it was the profound vocal virtuosity of the group, coupled with the obsession drive and compositional ambitions of their leader, Brian Wilson, that promised their survival after the eventual breaking of fad fever....

Comparison to other vocally oriented rock groups, such as the Association, shows the Beach Boys' technique to be far superior, almost embarrassingly so. They were so confident of their ability, and of Brian's skill as a producer to enhance it, that they were unafraid of doing sophisticated, a cappella glee-club arrangements containing multiple suspensions, passing formations, complex chords, and both chromatic and enharmonic modulations.

Influenced by doo-wop and rhythm and blues, they began as a garage band playing 1950s style rock and roll. During their early years, the Beach Boys released music that displayed an increasing level of sophistication, a period where Brian Wilson consistently acted as the group's primary bandleader, songwriter, producer, and arranger for the group's most commercially and critically successful work.

Together, the band reassembled styles of music such as surf to include vocal jazz harmony, creating their unique sound.

In addition, they introduced their signature approach to common genres such as the pop ballad by applying harmonic or formal twists not native to rock and roll. Miller observed, "On straight rockers they sang tight harmonies behind Love's lead ... on ballads, Brian played his falsetto off against lush, jazz-tinged voicings, often using (for rock) unorthodox harmonic structures."

Harrison adds, "But even the least distinguished of the Beach Boys' early up-tempo rock 'n' roll songs show traces of structural complexity at some level; Brian was simply too curious and experimental to leave convention alone." This new sound was quickly associated with the Modernism movement blooming in the Los Angeles music scene. The band later went on to incorporate many genres, from baroque pop to psychedelia and synthpop.

In early 1964, Brian began his breakaway from beach-themed music. Later in November of the same year, the group expressed desires to advance from the surf rock style for which they initially became known for. Experimentation with psychotropic substances proved pivotal to the group's development as artists. The following month, Brian was introduced to cannabis before quickly progressing to LSD in early 1965.

Of his first *acid* trip, Brian recalled that the drug had subjected him to "a very religious experience" which enlightened him to indescribable philosophies. The music for "California Girls", the first Beach Boys song Bruce Johnston participated in, came from this first LSD experience, as did much of the group's subsequent work where they would often partake in drug use during recording sessions.

Brian is quoted saying: "Everyone contributed something. Carl kept us hip to the latest tunes, Al taught us his repertoire of folk songs, and Dennis, though he didn't [initially] play anything, added a combustible spark just by his presence." Early on, Love sang lead vocals in the rock-oriented songs, while Carl contributed crisp guitar lines on the group's ballads. In a 1966 article that asks "Do the Beach Boys rely too much on sound genius Brian?"

Carl responded that every member of the group contributes ideas but admitted that Brian was majorly responsible for their music. In 1967, Dennis was cited as the "the closest to brother Brian's own musical ideals ... He always emphasizes the fusion, in their work, of pop and classical music."

The band's earliest influences came primarily from the work of Chuck Berry and the Four Freshmen. Performed by the Four Freshmen, "Their Hearts Were Full of Spring" (1961) was a particular favorite of the group. By deconstructing their arrangements of pop standards, Brian educated himself on jazz harmony. Taking this into mind, Philip Lambert noted, "If Bob Flanigan helped teach Brian how to sing, then Gershwin, Kern, Porter, and the other members of this pantheon helped him learn how to craft a song."

Other general influences on the group included the Hi-Los, the Penguins, the Robins, Bill Haley & His Comets, Otis Williams, the Cadets, the Everly Brothers, the Belmonts, the Shirelles, the Regents, and the Crystals.

While the Beach Boys are not often associated with blues, Brian has called this a misapprehension, citing Smokey Robinson and Stevie Wonder as influences. Regarding surf rock pioneer Dick Dale, Brian clarified that his influence on the group was limited to Carl and his style of guitar playing.

Carl himself named Berry, the Ventures, and John Walker for shaping his guitar style, and that the Beach Boys had learned to play all of the Ventures' songs by ear early in their career.

The influence of the Beach Boys' peers combined with Brian's competitive nature drove him to reach higher creative peaks. Sometime around late 1963, he heard the song "Be My Baby" (1963) by the Ronettes for the first time, revamping his creative interests and songwriting. "Be My Baby" is considered the epitome of *Phil Spector's* Wall of Sound production technique, a recording method that fascinated Wilson for the next several decades.

Brian later reflected: "I was unable to really think as a producer up until the time where I really got familiar with *Phil Spector's* work. That was when I started to design the experience to be a record rather than just a song." He kept "Be My Baby" on his living room jukebox and listened to it whenever the mood struck him.

According to engineer Larry Levine, "Brian was one of the few people in the music business Phil respected. There was a mutual respect. Brian might say that he learned how to produce from watching Phil, but the truth is, he was already producing records before he observed Phil. He just wasn't getting credit for it, something that in the early days, I remember really used to make Phil angry. Phil would tell anybody who listened that Brian was one of the great producers."

Other prominent inspirations for Brian included Gershwin's "Rhapsody in Blue" (1924), the Beatles' *Rubber Soul* (1965), and composer Burt Bacharach. Author Domenic Priore wrote that, in a subtle way, Brian grew to appreciate the potential of what a pop song could do after being partially spurred on by the dynamics of Bacharach's "Walk On By" (1964).

This song became as influential to him as "Be My Baby", supporting his strive to achieve a sense of dynamics in his recordings while he began pulling away from a purely Spector-inspired approach to production.

Brian supported this by saying, "Burt Bacharach and Hal David are more like me. They're also the best pop team – per se – today. As a producer, Bacharach has a very fresh, new approach."

Even though the Wilson family did not grow up in "a particularly religious household," Carl was described as "the most truly religious person I know" by Brian, and Carl was forthcoming about the group's spiritual beliefs stating: "We believe in God as a kind of universal consciousness. God is love. God is you. God is me.

God is everything right here in this room. It's a spiritual concept which inspires a great deal of our music." Carl told *Rave* magazine in 1967 that the group's influences are of a "religious nature", but not any religion in specific, only "an idea based upon that of Universal Consciousness. ... The spiritual concept of happiness and doing good to others is extremely important to the lyric of our songs, and the religious element of some of the better church music is also contained within some of our new work."

After being asked in a 1988 interview about whether his music is or was religiously influenced, Brian referred to the 1962-published *A Toehold on Zen* and said that he believed that he possessed what is called a "toehold," defined metaphorically as "any small step which allows one to move toward a greater goal." He elaborated, "I learned from that book and from people who had a toehold on... say somebody had a grasp on life, a good grasp—they ought to be able to transfer that over to another thing." During the recording of *Pet Sounds*, Brian held prayer meetings, later reflecting that "God was with us the whole time we were doing [the] album ... I could feel that feeling in my brain."

In 1966, he explained that he wanted to move into a white spiritual sound, and predicted that the rest of the music industry would follow suit. In 2011, Brian maintained the spirituality was important to his music, but that he did not follow any particular religion.

The Beach Boys included an interpretation of "The Lord's Prayer" as the B-side to their 1963 "Little Saint Nick" single. Brian expressed apprehensiveness over naming his song "God Only Knows" because, in the 1960s, references to God in pop music were largely unheard of.

Carl said that *Smile* was chosen as an album title because of its connection to the group's spiritual beliefs. Brian referred to *Smile* as his "teenage symphony to God", composing a hymn, "Our Prayer", as the album's opening spiritual invocation.

He spoke of his LSD trips as a "religious experience", and during a session for "Our Prayer", Brian can be heard asking the other Beach Boys: "Do you guys feel any acid yet?". In 1968, Mike Love's interest in transcendental meditation led the Beach Boys to record the original song "Transcendental Meditation".

Brian identified each member individually for their vocal range, once detailing the ranges for Carl, Dennis, Jardine ("[they] progress upwards through G, A, and B") Love ("can go from bass to the E above middle C"), and himself ("I can take the second D in the treble clef"). He declared in 1966 that his greatest interest was to expand modern vocal harmony, owing his fascination with voice to the Four Freshmen, which he considered a "groovy sectional sound."

He added, "The harmonies that we are able to produce give us a uniqueness which is really the only important thing you can put into records – some quality that no one else has got. I love peaks in a song – and enhancing them on the control panel. Most of all, I love the human voice for its own sake."

Rock critic Erik Davis wrote, "The 'purity' of tone and genetic proximity that smoothed their voices was almost creepy, pseudo-castrato, [and] a 'barbershop' sound." According to Brian: "Jack Good once told us, 'You sing like eunuchs in a Sistine Chapel,' which was a pretty good quote." For a period, Brian avoided singing falsetto for the group, saying "I thought people thought I was a fairy. ... The band told me, 'If that's the way you sing, don't worry about it."

From lowest intervals to highest, the group's vocal harmony stack usually began with Love or Dennis, followed by Jardine or Carl, and finally Brian on top. Jardine explains, "We always sang the same vocal intervals. ... As soon as we heard the chords on the piano we'd figure it out pretty easily.

If there was a vocal move [Brian] envisioned, he'd show that particular singer that move. We had somewhat photographic memory as far as the vocal parts were concerned so that never a problem for us."

Striving for absolute perfection, Brian's intricate vocal arrangements exercised the group's calculated blend of intonation, attack, phrasing, and expression. Sometimes, he would sing each vocal harmony part alone through multi-track tape. Jimmy Webb has said, "They used very little vibrato and sing in very straight tones. The voices all lie down beside each other very easily – there's no bumping between them because the pitch is very precise."

The group's instrumental combo initially involved Brian on bass guitar and keyboards, Carl on guitar, and Dennis on drums. From an early age, Brian demonstrated an extraordinary skill for learning music by ear on keyboard. Using major Hollywood recording studios, he arranged many of his compositions for a conglomerate of session musicians informally known as the Wrecking Crew.

Their assistance was needed due to the increasingly complicated nature of the material. As a result, a number of songs do not credit the Beach Boys as instrumentalists, but nearly invariably as lead, harmony, or backing vocalists. It's the belief of Richie Unterberger that, "Before session musicians took over most of the parts, the Beach Boys could play respectably gutsy surf rock as a self-contained unit."

In spite of this, Carl Wilson continued to play beside these musicians whenever he was available to attend sessions. In archivist Craig Slowinski's view, "One should not sell short Carl's own contributions; the youngest Wilson had developed as a musician sufficiently to play alongside the horde of high-dollar session pros that big brother was now bringing into the studio. Carl's guitar playing [was] a key ingredient."

Additionally, it is often erroneously stated that Dennis' drumming in the Beach Boys' recordings was filled in exclusively by studio musicians. His drumming is documented on a number of the group's singles, including "I Get Around", "Fun, Fun Fun", and "Don't Worry Baby".

Brian's experiments with his Wollensack tape recorder provide early examples of his flair for exotica and unusual percussive patterns and arranging ideas that he would recycle in later prominent work. Through attending Phil Spector's sessions sporadically, Brian learned how to act as a producer for records while being educated on the Wall of Sound process.

From then on, Brian received some production advice from Jan Berry. As they collaborated on several hit singles written and produced for other artists, they recorded what would later be regarded the California Sound.

The positive commercial response to Brian's structurally irregular and harmonically varied pop compositions gave him the prestige, resources, and courage to further his creative aspirations. He proceeded to explore many unusual combinations of instruments while emphasizing inventive percussion and progressively ambitious lyricism. Although he was often dubbed a perfectionist, Brian was an inexperienced musician, and his understanding was mostly self-taught.

Sometimes he wrote songs with melodic lines in different keys at the same time, which confused session musicians. In most cases, he was forced to rely on outside collaborators when it came to adding lyricism to his compositions. At this stage, Brian usually worked with band mate *Mike Love*, whose assertive persona provided youthful swagger that contrasted Brian's explorations in romanticism and sensitivity.

Luis Sanchez noted a pattern where Brian would spare surfing imagery when working with collaborators outside of his band's circle, in the examples "Lonely Sea" and "In My Room".

He preferred mixing live as performances were recorded, as opposed to mixing after the fact. He was open to changes suggested by others while recording, often taking advice and even incorporating apparent mistakes if they provided a useful or interesting alternative. He experimented with processed effects including varispeed, reverberation, slap back echo, and filtering signals through a Leslie speaker.

Lyric collaborator Tony Asher remembers that in the 1960s: "People would try whatever they could think of that was unexpected, just for its own sake...spend three days and call in a bunch of oboe players. Try an instrument just because nobody had ever used it, and in the end, it wasn't in the final mix. That never happened with Brian.

He did the same kind of experimenting, not to see if he could accidentally stumble onto something unique, but he did these unique things because that's what he wanted to hear. And most of the time, it ended up on the record." Once an instrumental track was completed, vocals would then be overdubbed by the group.

On *Surfin' U.S.A.* (1963), Brian began double tracking. As was practiced by other record producers from the 1960s, most of his mixes ended up in single-channel monaural, believing that varied stereo speaker placement took his control over the sound image away to the listener.

Once Britz assembled a preliminary recording setup, Brian would take over the console, directing the instrumentalists from the booth using an intercom or verbal gestures after supplying them with chord charts that were sometimes written incorrectly. According to some reports, even though Britz was responsible for setting up recording, Brian would then adjust his configuration to a large extent.

Asher adds: "As unorganized or even unproductive as he [Brian] could be in other situations, when he got into a recording session, you had the sense he had ideas that were gonna get away from him if he didn't get 'em done right away. He was willing to have people be relaxed and joke a little bit, but he wanted to get work done. And he sometimes lost his temper just a little bit if Chuck couldn't find a take."

At Gold Star Studios, Brian worked mainly with engineers Stan Ross and, with lesser frequency, Larry Levine. Ross said of Brian, "[he] liked the sound Gold Star got on the instrumentation, but he did the voices elsewhere because we were limited to two or three tracks and that wasn't enough for voice overdubbing. ... The tracks were really rhythm pads that would be sweetened after the voices were put on."

As Brian's productions advanced, he became recognized for his pop artistry, vocal harmonization, incessant studio perfectionism, forward-thinking song structures, engineering and mixing know-how, and creative multitasking abilities. It was unusual among rock groups that Brian wrote his own arrangements.

This included his own string orchestrations, which Asher referred to for their odd voicings and classical style. Session bassist Carol Kaye noted, "We had to create [instrumental] parts for all the other groups we cut for, but not Brian.

We were in awe of Brian." Friend Danny Hutton expressed similar feelings while highlighting Brian's studio proficiency, citing what he believed to be an extraordinary talent at harnessing several different studio spaces while piecing together discrete instrumental patterns and timbres cohesively.

He noted, "Somebody could go in right after Brian's session and try to record, and they could never get the sound he got. There was a lot of subtle stuff he did. ... People don't talk that much about it. They always talk about his music. He was fabulous in the studio, in terms of getting sounds. You'd sit there, and that was him. He was just hands-on. He would change the reverb and the echo, and all of a sudden, something just – *whoa!* – got twice as big and fat."

Foreshadowed by *Beach Boys' Party!* (1965), much of the group's recordings from 1967 to 1970 displayed sparse instrumentation, a more relaxed ensemble, and a seeming inattention to production quality. Brian briefly experimented with *musique concrete* and minimalist rock approaches to music before retreating to his home recording studio to record "manic" material in the 1970s, enacting syncopated exercises and counterpoints layered on jittery eighth note tone clusters and loping shuffle grooves.

During the infancy of Brian's home studio, the group was forced to improvise many technical aspects of recording. In one instance, they used an empty swimming pool as *an echo chamber.*

When Brian abdicated from the group, the other members were forced to take a more active production role. This is believed to have faltered the quality of their music. *Richie Unterberger* believes that after the December 1967 release of *Wild Honey*, "The Beach Boys were revealed as a group that, although capable of producing some fine and interesting music, were no longer innovators on the level of the Beatles and other figureheads."

The album marked the beginning of Carl's increased role as producer, who described it as "music for Brian to cool out by", signaling a mellower approach that pervaded into the 1970s. In 1968, Dennis contributed original songs to *Friends*, revealing himself as a broodingly soulful songwriter and singer, while Bruce Johnston devised a moody instrumental, "The Nearest Faraway Place", for *20/20* the following year.

Sunflower (1970) marked an end to the experimental songwriting and production phase initiated by *Smiley Smile* (1967). Of the albums between *Surf's Up* (1971) and *Holland* (1973), Daniel Harrison wrote that they "contain a mixture of middle-of-the-road music entirely consonant with pop style during the early 1970s with a few oddities that proved that the desire to push beyond conventional boundaries was not dead."

While Harrison adamantly states "1974 is the year in which the Beach Boys ceased to be a rock 'n' roll act and became an oldies act," *Love You* (1977) is perceived by some as an oddity that sounds like no other record in their catalog with synthesizer-laden arrangements played almost entirely by Brian.

Regarded by some critics as one of the greatest American rock groups and an important catalyst in the evolution of popular music, the Beach Boys are one of the most critically acclaimed, commercially successful, and widely influential bands of all time. The Beach Boys' sales estimates range from 100 to 350 million records worldwide and have influenced artists spanning many genres and decades.

Their early hits helped raise the profile of the state of California, creating its first major regional style with national significance, and establishing a musical identity for <u>Southern California</u>, as opposed to *Hollywood*. This also associated the band with surfing, *hot-rod* racing, and a contemporaneous teenage lifestyle and fantasy. Surf bands existed prior to the Beach Boys, but none projected a world view the way the Beach Boys did.

The resultant "California Sound" later morphed itself to reflect a more musically ambitious and mature world view, becoming less to do with surfing and cars and more about social consciousness and political awareness. Between 1964 and 1969, it fueled innovation and transition, inspiring artists to tackle largely unmentioned themes such as sexual freedom, black pride, drugs, oppositional politics, and war.

Brian's work is credited as a major innovation in the field of music production. According to Erik Davis, "Not only did the Beach Boys write a soundtrack to the early '60s, but Brian let loose a delicate and joyful art pop unique in music history and presaged the mellowness so fundamental to '70s California pop." *The A.V. Club* wrote that Brian was among "studio rats ... [that] set the pace for how pop music could and should sound in the Flower Power era: at once starry-eyed and wistful."

Only 21 years old when he received the freedom to produce his own records with total creative autonomy, he ignited an explosion of like-minded California producers, supplanting New York as the center of popular records, and becoming the first rock producer to use the studio as a discrete instrument. The Beach Boys were thus one of the first rock groups to exert studio control.

The group was among early (or earliest) instigators of psychedelic rock, acid rock, art rock, art pop, progressive rock, and sunshine pop. They attracted a following from a great number of their pop or rock contemporaries during the 1960s, including the Beatles, the Rolling Stones, Harry Nilsson, Cream, George Martin, the Who, Pink Floyd, Lou Reed of The Velvet Underground, and Frank Zappa.

Additionally, they influenced pioneering musicians for glam rock: David Bowie and Marc Bolan; krautrock: Faust, Kraftwerk; power pop: Big Star; and new wave: Talking Heads.

In the 1990s, the Beach Boys received a resurgence of popularity with alternative rock groups and young record-buyers of independent music. According to Sean O'Hagan of the High Llamas, "[they] stopped listening to indie records" in favor of the Beach Boys.

Bands who advocated for the band included founding members of the Elephant 6 Collective: Neutral Milk Hotel, the Olivia Tremor Control, the Apples in Stereo, and of Montreal. United by a shared love of the Beach Boys' music, they named Pet Sounds Studio in honor of the group.

Other influenced artists who gained prominence in underground circles during the 1980s and 1990s include shoe gaze band My Bloody Valentine, electronic outfits Daft Punk, Saint Etienne, The High Llamas, the Avalanches, Stereo lab, and alternative rock musicians Radiohead, Sonic Youth, Frank Black of Pixies, Jim Reid of the Jesus and Mary Chain, and Paddy McAloon of Prefab Sprout. In Japan, their music affected the work of noise rock bands Seagull Screaming Kiss Her Kiss Her and Melt-Banana.

Other 20th century artists influenced by the Beach Boys include

ABBA, Rivers Cuomo of Weezer, Fleetwood Mac, Cheap Trick, Chicago, Elton John, Flipper's Guitar, Todd Rundgren, Keiichi Suzuki, Yo La Tengo, Tatsuro Yamashita, Yellow Magic Orchestra, and XTC. The Beach Boys' influence has continued to pervade in such millennial artists as Air, Animal Collective, Fleet Foxes, MGMT, Super Furry Animals, and Frank Ocean.

Professor of cultural studies James M. Curtis wrote in 1987:

"… we can say that the Beach Boys represent the outlook and values of white Protestant Anglo-Saxon teenagers in the early sixties. Having said that, we immediately realize that they must mean much more than this. Their stability, their staying power, and their ability to attract new fans prove as much."

Historian Darren R. Reid added in 2013, "Imagine, if you will, a world in which the Beatles were known only for their early hits whilst *The White Album* or *Abbey Road* were of interest, or even known, only to the group's biggest fans, and you will have some grasp of how the Beach Boys' distorted public image has helped to *bury* their most important artistic works."

Throughout their career, the Beach Boys struggled with their public image and audiences. Musicologist Charlie Gillett explains, "By 1965, the Beach Boys had become an American pop institution, but although they continued to cultivate a visual image in line with their name and early repertoire, there was a limit to how many different ways Wilson could celebrate the wonders of living in Southern California.

Originally, many serious pop fans dismissed the group as trashy pop for kids." Their growing complexity caused their live performances to suffer in the mid 1960s, when the group began to be derided by audiences for their uniformed striped shirts compounded by low key reproductions of songs that required complicated orchestrations.

Because of their early hits, which celebrated a politically unconscious youth culture, the group's legitimacy in rock music became an oft-repeated criticism toward the band. In 1970, the group ceased wearing matching uniforms on stage and began emphasizing political and social awareness. Drawing from their associations with *Charles Manson a*nd Ronald Reagan, Erik Davis observed, "The Beach Boys may be the only bridge between those deranged poles.

There is a wider range of political and aesthetic sentiments in their records than in any other band in those heady times—like the state [of California], they expand and bloat and contradict themselves."

Despite the group's immense popularity and success, some consider that the extent of their contribution to Western music canon is undervalued. In 1967, Lou Reed famously wrote, "Will none of the powers that be realize what Brian Wilson did with *the chords*?" Pitchfork Media posited, "At some point, you learn that the Beach Boys weren't just a fun 1960s surf band with a run of singles that later came to be used in commercials; at their best, they were making capital-A Art.

Once you've absorbed [*Pet Sounds*], you find yourself going back through songs like "Don't Worry Baby", "The Warmth of the Sun", and "I Get Around", finding a deeper brilliance where you once heard only pop craftsmanship."

Discussing the 2011 release of *The Smile Sessions*, *The Los Angeles Times* wrote, "…certainly every library of American recording history needs this; university composition departments, music professors, budding recording engineers and composers should study it."

"I think a lot of critics punish the band for not going beyond 'Good Vibrations' … I think they love the band so much that they get crazy because we don't top ourselves. … every time there's a new Beach Boy record it competes with so many old Beach Boy records on the radio. … the audience is so young and they're reacting more to the Beach Boys sound-alike commercials on TV and the three or four really big, quadruple platinum repackage albums. I'm not down on any of that stuff, but … growth in this business is tough."
—*Bruce Johnston speaking to the Houston Chronicle, August 1982*

(Citation): Online publication *NewMusicBox*—which normally covers new American music outside the commercial mainstream—argued that the Beach Boys could never earn themselves "the same pride of place in American music history held by other great innovators" because of their mistaken reputation as a "light-hearted party band that drooled over California Girls while on a Surfing Safari," hampered not only by the over-saturation of their early songs being used in film, commercials, and other media, but also "...their latter-day cover-band-version-of-their-former-selves concert appearances."

Referring to the groups' reaction to the commercial success of their 1974 greatest hits compilation *Endless Summer*, Daniel Harrison writes, "they returned to the beach, knowing they would never leave it again."

Erik Davis wrote that by 1990, "the Beach Boys are either dead, deranged, or dinosaurs; their records are Eurocentric, square, unsampled; they've made too much money to merit hip revisionism." From the same period, Jim Miller wrote, "They have become a figment of their own past, prisoners of their unflagging popularity—incongruous emblems of a sunny myth of eternal youth belied by much of their own best music. ... The group is still largely identified with its hits from the early Sixties."

He explains, "The spirit of experimentation is just as palpable in *Smiley Smile* as it is in, say, Schoenberg's op. 11 piano pieces." While the group "went into the great void beyond", such notions were not widely acknowledged by rock audiences nor by the classically minded at the time. Harrison concludes: "What influences could these innovations then have?

The short answer is, not much. *Smiley Smile*, *Wild Honey*, *Friends*, and *20/20* sound like few other rock albums; they are *sui generis*. ... It must be remembered that the commercial failure of the Beach Boys' experiments was hardly motivation for imitation. In the end, we must conclude that the Beach Boys' late-1960s experiments were not reproducible."

The group routinely appears in the upper reaches of ranked lists such as "The Top 1000 Albums of All Time." Many of the group's songs and albums including *The Beach Boys Today!* (1965), *Smiley Smile* (1967), *Sunflower* (1970), and *Surf's Up* (1971) are featured in several lists devoted to the greatest of all time.

The 1966 releases *Pet Sounds* and *Good Vibrations* frequently rank among the top of critics' lists of the greatest albums and singles of all time. In 2004, *Pet Sounds* was preserved in the National Recording Registry by the Library of Congress for being "culturally, historically, and aesthetically significant."

Their recordings of "In My Room", "Good Vibrations", "California

Girls" and the entire *Pet Sounds* album have been inducted into the Grammy Hall of Fame.[411] On Acclaimed Music, "Good Vibrations" is ranked the third best song of all time, while "God Only Knows" is ranked twenty-first; the group itself is ranked eleven in its 1000 most recommended artists of all time.

In 1966 and 1967, reader polls conducted by the UK magazine *NME* crowned the Beach Boys as the world's number one vocal group, ahead of the Beatles and the Rolling Stones. In 1974, the Beach Boys were awarded "Band of the Year" by Rolling Stone. On December 30, 1980, the Beach Boys were awarded a star on the Hollywood Walk of Fame, located at 1500 Vine Street. The group was inducted into the Rock and Roll Hall of Fame in 1988.

Ten years later they were selected for the Vocal Group Hall of Fame. In 2001, the group received a Grammy Lifetime Achievement Award. In 2004, *Rolling Stone* ranked the Beach Boys number 12 on its list of the 100 Greatest Artists of All Time. Brian Wilson was inducted into the UK Rock and Roll Hall of Fame in November 2006.

The Wilsons' California house, where the Wilson brothers grew up and the group began, was demolished in 1986 to make way for Interstate 105, the Century Freeway. A *Beach Boys Historic Landmark* (California Landmark No. 1041 at 3701 West 119th Street), dedicated on May 20, 2005, marks the location.

The Beach Boys appear as performers in the beach party films *The Girls on the Beach* (1965) and *The Monkey's Uncle* (1965). They have also made cameo appearances in the television series *Full House* (1988–1992), *Home Improvement* (1993), and *Baywatch* (1995).

The life of the Beach Boys is the subject of two made-for-television films: *Summer Dreams: The Story of the Beach Boys* (1990) and *The Beach Boys: An American Family* (2000). *Love & Mercy* is a 2014 biopic that dramatizes Brian Wilson during his time with the Beach Boys.

Charlie decided to take a trip down Memory Lane, musically speaking that is. He has been doing this a lot lately now that he is getting older, no, not senile, at least he prays that is not the case. He looked up the acknowledged SCSM (Southern California Surfer Music) Pioneers, The *Beach Boys*, on the Internet (Charlie says that you can find anything on the Net these days, anything). Recently he even looked himself (Charles 'Charlie' Warner Kennedy O'Brien) up just for fun and to see what it said about him.

He was surprised that there was a whole lot of information on him posted to the Internet. Information like that he was a worldwide Private Investigator (Private Detective or Private Eye) and that he had been a Detective for the LAPD (Los Angeles Police Department) for 20 years. And, that he lives in the exclusive Huntington Harbor area located in the city of Huntington Beach in the OC (Orange County, California).

The Internet also listed his home address, unlisted land line phone number and his private cell phone number. Charlie was very, very upset about this to say the least. He deals with and apprehends heinous criminals, murderers, drug cartel members and other vile crooks and bad guys on a regular basis as part of his quite dangerous vocation (a Private Eye).

He was not a happy camper that any of these bad apples could just look him up on the Net and pay him an unexpected visit at his home to rearrange some or all of his old bones, remove some of his needed body parts, or set a IED to greet him as he opened his door/alarm which would send his body pieces flying all over Newport Beach. He made a mental note to contact one of the privacy companies to have all of his personal information removed as soon as he had some time.

Anyway, after he read about himself on the Net, calmed himself down a little bit, he continued to read up on his two-other favorite 'original founders' of Surf Rock founders, singer-song writers, namely ...

Charlie likes the newer popular singers, song writers and groups that he mentioned previously, however, as you already know, he is *old school* and still likes to *reminisce* about the good old days when he was younger, smarter, stronger and still Tall, dark and handsome. Well, he said to himself, "Charlie at least you are still tall. And one out of six ain't that bad."

EIGHT

THE PRESIDENT OF 'The Bank of Orange County' called Charlie and he sounded quite worried as well as very upset. He had met Charlie before, back when Charlie had helped the Bank out and put an end to the Banks' 'crime spree' and robberies of its 13-branch chain.

He informed Charlie that 'Thomas Rose', the Chairman of the Banks' Board, and his lovely wife, Pamela, were on a much-needed vacation, in 'Rosa Rita' Beach (located close to Ensenada), in Baja California, Mexico.

It is one of the most beautiful and pristine beaches on the California Coast line, that runs from the famous and exquisite vacation spot of 'Cabo San Lucas', Mexico to the pretty and artistic-looking bay of San Francisco. Out of the blue, they had been Kidnapped and were being held for a $3,000,000 ransom.

Also, the ransom note stated that unless it was paid in cash, and immediately, the body parts of Thomas and Pamela would be sent back to the Bank, one *piece* at a time.

The Roses were staying at a very exclusive resort and golf course named, 'Hermosa Beach Villa's and Country Club.' Hermosa means Beautiful in Spanish and believe me folks this place was extremely beautiful, it truly was. The cost was $1,500 per night for the best room with the best views. And that was the one Tom wanted for his pretty wife, of course.

Also, that was very reasonable for this gorgeous and right on the beach location suite with the professionally designed golf course (by Jordan Speith), the terrific rooms with large Jacuzzis in the bathrooms, 2,000 square feet, mind-blowing ocean views and professional tennis courts designed by Serena Williams (the Tennis Great from Southern California). FYI - Charlie loved to watch her play and has been rooting for her ever since she first started playing tennis back in the day.

Also, this place had full body spas open 24/7, FIFA inspired soccer fields, a Heli - spot, beach cabanas all along the beach with open air bars and live entertainment all day and all night as well as renowned concierge service that could provide the guests with anything that their little hearts desired. And I do mean anything.

The fabulous Hermosa Hotel had numerous very well-trained and armed Security Guards (from Securitas Security International located in Sweden), as well as several armed 'undercover' security guards. The plain clothes guards wore tourists' clothing and blended in well with all of the vacation guests.

Some in shorts, Mexican T-Shirts, Huarache sandals and some women guards even in little tiny bikinis (Charlie was not sure where they hid their guns) and others with big sombreros, of course, as it was Mexico, after all.

The 'Hermosa Beach Villas and County Club' had recently hired several additional armed guards in addition to the ones that they already had (about 15), because hundreds of American (and other International Tourists) had been Threatened, robbed at gun/knife point, with women humiliated and assaulted, men beaten to an inch of their lives and even more frightening, many were Kidnapped and held for ransom.

The International Newspapers were warning tourists not to go to Baja California, or Mexico, at this time due the imminent threat of serious personal violence. They called the Baja, the 'Kidnap Capitol' of the world with Columbia, South America, as number two in these types of Heinous Crimes.

This news and information made Charlie extremely sad. He loved Baja California and its great people and he had been going there since he was a 16-year-old kid. He favored Tijuana (on the border) Mexico for a long time but for the past 15 years, he has preferred the quiet and serenity of Ensenada.

Charlie saw a quite disturbing article in his favorite newspaper, the LA (Los Angeles) Times. The subject article read as Herewith:

U. S. ISSUES NEW TRAVEL WARNING

"The U.S. State Department updated its travel warning for Mexico by including three additional states on its list of places it recommends Americans avoid when south of the border. The new warning adds the northern state of Tamauilpas, northern Pacific coast state of Sinaloa, and the western state of Michoacán, noting that all three are troubled by organized crime and drug violence.

The U.S. State Department previously had warned against traveling to the northern states of Baja California, Chihuahua, Durango, and Coahuila also crime and drug hot spots."

The Mexican National Federales (Policia = Police) in Mexico City said that the "Sinaloa Drug Cartel" was most likely behind most of these Horrific criminal activities. Also, that it's Jefe (leader) was none other than the Infamous Joaquin 'El Chapo' Guzman Loera. El Chapo in Spanish means Shorty. He was only 5'5" but with a stocky build, strong as a Bull and had black daggers for eyes. He had previously broken out of the two most secure prisons in all of Mexico, in the USA, what we call Super Max Prisons. He broke out once in 1991 and again in 2015.

El Chapo's five top *Pistoleros* and Lieutenants were: Gonzalo Pedro Garcia (El Toro = the Bull) who put fear into all of those around him. Javier Fernandez Santiago (the Horse) - People felt that he would stampede on their heads at the drop of the hat. Alvaro Fernando Martinez (the Serpent) who bites just like a rattlesnake but without the warning or rattle. Felipe Isidoro Carillo (El Coche = the Car) who ran over his enemies with his own car, a new black Chevy SS Camero.

And, Alejandro Jorge Alvarez (the Blade) who was lightening quick with his big knife and cut people up before they even had time to draw their guns. El Chapo had hundreds of other 'foot soldiers', of course, but these were the ones in charge of the Kidnappings, Tortures, and collecting of the ominous Ransoms, for the much-feared and hated 'Sinaloa Drug Cartel'.

Charlie immediately did a lot of research on the rash of kidnappings in Mexico, and especially in Baja California. He found out that the EPR, Ejecito Popular Revolucionario (the Popular Revolutionary Army), or the, EZLN, Ejecito Zapatista de Liberacion National the Zapata National Liberation Army) were the two other possible candidates to have pulled off the extremely dangerous and very risky kidnapping of an American citizen who was the Chairman of a major Bank and his wife.

Even with all of the kidnappings in Mexico, no group had ever kidnapped anyone with such a high Profile. That told Charlie that whoever did this dastardly deed was very well-funded and not at all afraid of the Mexican nor the U.S. Government.

The suspected leaders of the EPR are Isidoro Jorje Fernandez (the Comandante = General) and his lovely wife, Carmen Luisa Carrillo (the Field Captain). They are both thought to be about 30 years old, albeit, little is known about them. They are said to be from Chiapas, or Tlaxcala, in southern Mexico. The EPR is larger, better-funded and much more heavily armed than the EZLN.

It would have been much easier for the EPR to carry out this extremely difficult kidnap and covert operation. The EZLN, however, needs money very badly to carry on their Liberation Movement. Also, this crime would give them a lot of much-needed cash, as well as publicity and national TV coverage.

The PDPR-EPR (Partido Democratico Popular Revolucionario-Ejecito Popular Revolucion Ario) is the militarized wing of the political party of the EPR and it purports to have a Maoist Theology and advocates a socialist peasant revolution inside of Mexico. They have been in existence since June 28, 1996. On that date they published their "Agus Blancas Manifesto."

Their goal is the overthrow of the duly-elected Mexican Government. The PDPR-EPR does not function in the political world independent of the EPR (by itself). And, the party does not appear on election ballots in Mexico at this time, either at the local levels (where they are very popular) nor the State or Federal levels.

The EPR raises most of their money for anti-government funding by

'Kidnapping' one of the following: Vacationing Norte Americanos (North Americans-US Citizens) or U.S. businessmen and women who live and work in Mexico or wealthy Mexican nationals (local Citizens).

They have no problem taking advantage of their own public when it comes to making money. The EZLN is loosely associated with the EPR. It is said to be run by a man called "Subcomandante Marcos." He is thought not to be quite as radical and violent as the leaders of the EPR. He is believed to be from either Oaxaca, or Guanajuato, also in southern Mexico.

Marcos always wears a black ski mask when he speaks in public or on Video Communications. Only his closest associates know his real name, what he looks like, or anything about him. Some people refer to the EZLN as "Zapatistas" for short.

Immediately after he had accepted this urgent and difficult case, Charlie jumped on a 'Aero Mexicana' small jet plane and flew to the Ensenada Regional Airport. As soon as he landed, he went to Enterprise Car Rental and pick up the car he had previously ordered. It was an almost brand -new European Silver BMW 535i Grand Turismo Luxury Sedan, with a specially designed racing engine.

He felt that with this scary case, in this crime-ridden part of Mexico and with these very dangerous drug cartel members, he might very well need some High Output V-8 horsepower to make a fast getaway if he was outnumbered by the Bad guys. Or, if he was in 'hot' pursuit of one of them, he wanted to be able to catch them. They all drove fast cars, or big 4 x 4's with big engines.

The first thing that Charlie did was check in with the local Rosa Rita Policia (Police) Department's Chief of Policia (Diego 'El Diego' Hurtado Munguia - nickname 'Little Diego'). The word around town was that he was a good and honest man.

Charlie wanted to get a list from him of the Key Players in the Mexican Law Enforcements and Mexican Government, areas that might be able to assist him with Recovery of the Chairman of the Bank and his wife. He said to himself, "Charlie, time is extremely crucial in this case and the Clock is ticking." And, "you are going to need all of the help you can get, and you will need to get it fast, real fast."

Little Diego was well aware of the brazen Kidnapping and was very embarrassed that it happened in his Town and Under his Watch. He told Charlie that he would do anything to assist him, and then added, "Mi casa es su casa." Then he got on his computer and in a flash, hit the print button.

And just like magic, the print out appeared. The list that Little Diego provided to Charlie is presented herewith:

- Mexican Navy Rear Admiral 'Hermano Eduardo Alarcon (cousin of Raul and Fidel Castro of Cuba)
- Mexican Army (and Air Force) Four Star General 'Pedro Luis Zendajas'
- The FEDERALES (Mexican Federal/National Police) - Like the FBI in the States. Commandante 'Camineo Raphael Cardenas'
- Baja California (Including Ensenada and Rosa Rita Beach) - Governor 'Raul Gamboa Cedillo'
- Baja California State Attorney General 'Maria Guerro Villareal'
- Ensenada Chief of Policia (Police) 'Cueto Chacon Leon'

Charlie was quite impressed with Little Diego as well as his great attitude and fast assistance to the request. Charlie liked him already, and said to himself, "Charlie, this guy is going to be a big help to you in this challenging and difficult Kidnap Recovery case, a very big help."

The next thing Charlie had to do was go check into the Five Star Hotel at which he had reservations. Remember, the cost was covered on his expense account, so he wanted to go First Class, of course.

Right after hanging up his encrypted cell phone with his friend Howard, Charlie called his old Amigo Manuel 'Manny' Murrieta. Manny was related to the infamous or famous, 'Joaquin Murrieta', the quite well-known Bandito from the old days around Mexicali, and the Baja California area, in Mexico. Manny used to work for Howard, at the CIA, and was one of Howard's best field agents/operatives, as well as one of

Howard's closest friends.

Manny had also worked with the Federales (Mexico's National Police), and the USA -DEA (Drug Enforcement Agency) in Tijuana and Lower California while he was with the CIA and knew lots of the locals there. Charlie felt that these contacts could be very valuable in his search and rescue operation.

Manny was definitely Charlie's kind of man. He was street smart, very tough, quick-witted, a weapons expert, had the 'gift of gab' with people and more importantly he knew Ensenada and Baja California like the back of his hand. Manny now works as a Private Detective out of a nice, but smaller, office in Tijuana, Mexico.

Charlie could speak "un poquito Espanola" (little bit of Spanish), but not enough for this operation in Ensenada, there was no question about it. Manny could speak fluent Spanish, some local Mexican dialects, English and also some French.

And he knew how to keep his mouth shut and listen and see everything. He would be of great assistance in locating the kidnappers and, prayerfully, rescuing the hostages unharmed.

Charlie told Manny that he needed three very street smarts, strong and intelligent women PI's (Private Investigators) to assist them with this assignment. In other words, boots on the *ground*, as they say in the military.

He told Manny, that he was going to call them 'Charlie's Angels' just for fun. Manny told Charlie that he liked the ring of that, and that it reminded him of the old TV show, Charlie's Angels, from the 1970s.

Then he asked Manny if he knew of any former Mexican Policia (Police), DEA, or CIA women who are currently PIs in Baja, California. Manny immediately stated that he knew of three women PIs who would be perfect for the locating and rescuing operation. He listed them in a text that he sent to Charlie which read as follows:

Leticia 'Lettie' Cabrillo Montez - Charlie described Lettie to Howard (CIA) as being very well-educated from the "Mexican International Private University", a two-hundred-year-old and very well-respected college in Mexico City (population 15 million).

She earned a Bachelor of Arts Degree in Criminal Justice and she was quite articulate in conversations with criminals, drug cartel members, as well as people from other law enforcement agencies in Mexico and also the United States.

Lettie also had great computer skills to do the necessary reports that Charlie had to submit to the CIA, his customer, the Bank and his new friend, the Chief of Police in Rosa Rita Beach. And she knew how to send confidential and encrypted satellite communications to the CIA as well as other places.

Lettie was also very nice-looking with a great figure as well as quite high intelligence.

Plus, she was very discriminating, honest and trustworthy. Also, she had a good way with people, a very likeable personality and she was quite friendly. Of course, she could be as tough as nails and very effective when it came time to 'take care of business'. Charlie felt that Lettie would be very crucial to this extremely dangerous and complicated Search and Rescue assignment.

Maria Gabbana 'Gabby' Arnez - She was an expert in working with CI's (confidential informants). She was born in Mexico City and was fluent in Spanish, of course, and also English as well as Italian. She looked like a model, nice long legs (Charlie just loves long legs as you already know) with very pretty dark brown eyes.

Charlie felt that those physical attributes would help her to gather important and necessary intelligence information from CI's as well as other individuals. Charlie told Howard that he would tell her everything he knew if he were a criminal after she showed him those lovely long legs, if you know what he means.

A naturally attractive Latina woman, she could exude a voice as cold as a Siberian winter when it was needed. Charlie wants you to know, folks, that it is cold, real, real cold. And yet, when she wanted to, she could laugh in a delightful manner and her smile, when she wanted, could be as bright as a Shining Star.

When Gabby walked by, all of the men and I do mean all of the men... looked at her as she moved her great curves and made the earth move beneath her lovely legs. Just like a fashion model on the Italian Cat walk in Milan, or in Paris, France. Charlie told Manny that Gabby would be a great asset to our locating and rescuing case.

Angel Ortega 'Lulu' Bermudez was said to be an expert at running the internal control panel for the 'Reaper' as well as the 'Rapture' CIA surveillance *Drone*. And she was fluent in Spanish, English, and French. She was young, only 25, but wise beyond her years. Lulu was a very sharp cookie and pretty, too. Charlie thought that was a good combination for the dangerous operation they were about to embark on.

Also, she was very brave, too brave for her own good, perhaps. Angel was no petite miss, she was 5' 8" and she could handle herself quite well in hand to hand combat. Also, she was cool as an ice cube under pressure and also under fire (fire fights, etc.).

Very few men would suspect that this fit and trim woman packaged with all of those lush curves and the lovely long hair and miles of long legs could be so lethal, but she was one tough woman, as evidenced from the AK-47 automatic rifle she wore strapped across her camo suit, when she was on the job, or going into the field of battle.

Now, after Charlie had hired his new PI's (Private Investigators) namely 'Charlie's Angels', he and his new Lieutenant Manny Marietta, still needed a few good men (four men to be exact). They were needed for back up and also for added fire power for the upcoming search and rescue mission of the Bank CEO and his wife.

The men they selected after a long and detailed search are listed herewith:

Numero uno (number one)

Silverio Eduardo Alacon also known as The Tiger. He could pounce upon a man in less than 20 seconds and you would not even see him coming. Also, his mind and trigger finger were as quick as his body.

Numero dos (number two)

Lorenzo Calderone Vicente Fox, aka The Fox, naturally. He was as crafty as a fox just like the foxes he was nicknamed after. Also, he was a meticulous tracker in the outdoors and the mountains in the Baja California peninsula. This should come in very handy where they going on this mission and where they suspected the kidnappers were hiding out with the hostages.

Numero tres (number three)

Florencio Jose Diaz, aka, The Cheeta. He could spring into action on a moment's notice. Like, as an example, going from being sound asleep, to getting wide awake, dressed for action, armed to the teeth and ready for war in less than five minutes, flat.

Numero cuatro (number four)

Reynaldo Hernandez de Garcia, aka, The Magician. He could make people disappear, and so they said, "These people never come back after a visit from the Magician." Y mas importante (and more important) he was good and very handy with Malleable Plastique Explosives.

Charlie thought to himself, "Need I wish for any better men?" He did not think that he and Manny would be able to get four combats trained and hardened men half as efficient and professional as these men for his dangerous assault and rescue team.

Then, with some great CI (confidential informant) work by one of his Charlie's Angels and also Little Diego (Local Police Chief), Charlie was informed that the Sinaloa Drug Cartel Had Taken (Kidnapped) the Bank Chairman and his wife. That Cartel was still run by the infamous 'El Chapo' Guzman even though he just recently escaped from the most secure Federal prison in all of Mexico. He is one of the richest men in the whole wide world and said to be worth Billions and Billions of dollars.

Smuggling drugs into the USA from Columbia, South America was the Cartel's main earning power, however, they also made vast sums of money from Kidnapping for Ransom foreigners from many countries and visitors from America as well as their own citizens.

Charlie also learned that some of El Chapo's gang was holding the Bank CEO and his spouse at a famous local hideout called "Ranchito Diablo" (the Devils Ranch). It was located high up above the hills overlooking Ensenada. The mountain top enclave, or cattle ranch, had a completely unobstructed 360-degree view of all of the roads and even foot trails that lead up to the virtual Fortress.

The bad guys, and I mean really bad cartel members, would be able to see anyone, including Charlie and his assault and rescue team, for miles before they even got close to the Ranchito. Charlie pondered this serious dilemma, and then said to himself, "Drones, Charlie, use drones for the attack and rescue."

Then Charlie called Lulu (one of his Charlie Angels) and told her to call Howard at the CIA and order two Rapture Drones from his personal Armory. He wanted both of them equipped with several missiles as well at two .50 caliber high powered machine guns. That should wake up the criminals and their pistoleros at the hideout early some morning soon and Charlie thought, "Wake them up but good."

Lulu told Charlie Howard would 'hand' deliver the two Drones on a CIA cargo jet (a C-190 a big plane) in just two days. Also, Howard said to her, "Tell Charlie that his old buddy wants to go on the rescue mission with him." He said it sounded like fun and he was sick of being stuck in the office so much these days.

Charlie, when Lulu conveyed Howard's message, said, "Great, the more the merrier." Howard was a highly trained CIA field operative/agent for many years before being promoted to the CIA Director.

Now, Charlie had his right-hand man, Manny, his good pal Howard, his three Charlie's Angels, his new mini-army of four mercs (mercenaries), and his new BFF (best friend forever) Little Diego (Police Chief) who had volunteered for the assault.

Diego had told Charlie, "This vile kidnapping happened in my city, and on my watch, therefore, I most definitely want to be in on the action and rescue attempt, no matter how dangerous it will be."

Then Charlie said to himself, "I now have as good a small army (ten people) as anyone in all of Mexico, or even the US of A, for that matter."

At 0400 (Four AM) on Friday morning, Charlie and his *Magnificent Ten* search and rescue team, were already parked in two jet black Chevy Suburban SUV's (with bullet proof glass and a reinforced steel body), at the bottom of the hill directly below the "Ranchito Diablo." And then they saw them, but they could not hear the muffled motors of the *Rapture Drones* as they flew low and right over their heads as they stood outside of their SUV's.

Before the deadly Drones flew overhead, it was so quiet up in these rolling hills that you could hear a single bird chirp, a bald eagle flaps its long wings, or a coyote crying out in the night. There was also just a slight summer breeze blowing in off of the royal blue Pacific Ocean that was very close by.

Charlie had a big smile on his face, even though he was still half asleep, and he said out loud so the whole team could hear him, "Wake up time bad guys. You are about to have a bad day, a very, very bad day." Then he smiled a big smile and they all smiled back at him.

Then, Charlie took his three Charlie's Angels up the steep hill on the foot path leading to the west side of the Ranchito. There was a guard tower perched on top of the fence, watching the west side of the fortress.

It had two narcotraficantes on night guard duty and both had AK-47's with them at their ready. And just as they reached the summit (a quite formidable climb I might add), the .50 caliber guns on the Drones took out the two guards, permanently. Then Charlie and his Angels hastily cut a hole through the barbed wire fence and then carefully, very carefully, entered the compound.

At the same time, which was prearranged by Charlie, Manny along with Silverio (one of the good foot soldiers) went up the east side of the highly guarded fortress. There was also another guard tower located on that side with two more thugs in it.

One had a Mossberg military shotgun, and the other one had an M-15 automatic machine gun with a grenade launcher attached to it. Then the second of the deadly Drones eliminated them both at almost the exact same time as the first Drone took out the two guards on Charlie's west side.

Howard, along with Lorenzo (foot soldier) went up the long, winding hill, on the north side all the way to the top. Only one guard was standing duty there, as the hill was too steep to climb, or so they thought.

And, he was sound asleep, therefore, Howard did not want to kill him, so he just shot him with a Tranquilizer gun, and put him to sleep until morning. Night, night bad guy, Howard said to him as he slumped to the hard ground.

Little Diego, along with Florencio and Reynaldo (the two remaining foot soldiers) climbed up the south side to get to the hideout. That was the main gate and entrance, therefore, there were four armed guards stationed there. They were standing by the heavy reinforced metal gate to make sure that no one entered who was not supposed to get in.

Diego took out the two guards armed with AK-47's that were closest to him, and Florencio and Reynaldo eliminated the remaining two guards who were both carrying military type shot guns. They got to the front gate, and dispatched with the bad guys, at the same time the silent killers (the Drones) did away with both guard towers, perfect timing, just as Charlie had planned. Good job Charlie.

Then, as all Hades broke loose in the Ranchito and with the gunmen running around yelling, "We are being attacked by the Federales (the Mexican National Police). They have come to rescue the hostages. Kill them, kill them all."

Then, Charlie's friends (the Drones) were back, and this time they shot sidewinder missiles into the Armory, the vehicle buffer yard, the ammo dump, two barns and the big bunk house were most of the pistoleros were sleeping off a night of drinking Tequila (with worms).

The infra-red night vision cameras on the Drones (which gave marvelously clear photos) had already identified the out-building where the Roses were being held. To make sure that their missiles, or the machine guns, did not hit or damage them, they did a wonderful job of avoiding that building, but destroying all of the rest of the Ranchito. The drug Cartel would have to find a new hideout, this one was no longer in any condition to operate out of, thanks to Howard's Drones, of course.

Then Little Diego, who was a great help to Charlie from start to fin-

89

ish with this kidnapping and rescue operation, arrested the 15 surviving Sinaloa drug cartel members. Five of which were wounded, not seriously though, and 15 other bad guys were sent to the Maker (Dios=God) to judge them.

Charlie never judges people, good or bad people, he says, "All I can do is dispatch them, but only if I have to and then I let God sort them out." We hear you, Charlie. We hear you loud and clear.

After that, Diego, and the four great foot soldiers (e.g., Silverio, Lorenzo, Florencio and Reynaldo) handcuffed and led the 15 prisoners down the steep hill to a big diesel police truck that he had ordered to pick up the captives and take them to a secure prison in Mexico City. Diego said that the jails, and prisons, in Baja California were too easy for the wealthy drug cartels to break their comrades out of.

Charlie was absolutely ecstatic, he truly was. None of his ten-member search and rescue team were killed, and only he, Lulu (one of his Angels), and Manny were wounded by flying metal debris from the Drone missile targets. Thank you, Dios (God) Charlie prayed to himself.

Then Charlie took Thomas and Pamela Rose safely (and all in one piece, thank God) back to the airport so that they could fly back to the John Wayne airport in the OC. After Charlie waved goodbye to the Bank's CEO, and his lovely wife at the airport, he said to himself, but out loud this time, "You're the man, Charlie, and you still got it. Another successful assignment accomplished and completed." Then he added, "Just a walk in the park, or another day at the office." After which he smiled to himself, a great big smile.

NINE

AS SOON AS CHARLIE got back to the OC (Orange County) from his terrifying, extremely dangerous, yet thank God, successful rescue of Thomas Rose (Chairman and CEO of 'The Bank of Orange County') and his sweet wife, Pamela. He *pondered his rescue* (he tries to plan and ponder a lot during his investigations and let his inner spirit assist him with his very difficult and dangerous cases) and then contacted Joe Johnson at the City of Anahcim.

He told Joe that he had been out of town working on a quite serious kidnapping case in Mexico and had just returned that day.

And that he was now ready to finalize the Donald 'Bumpy' Bump investigation for the City of Anaheim. Also, he told Joe that he was sorry (La cento = sorry in Spanish) about the slight delay. Joe told Charlie that he was very happy that he had survived the *'Rosa Rita Beach'* rescue and was also glad he was back on the Donald's case.

Now, Charlie reviewed, and refreshed, in his mind and from his good notes, the whole case from the beginning. He recalled that he had felt from the 'get go' that the Death Threats were from either, a) a disgruntled former real estate client, or, b) a 'jilted' old girlfriend, and/or still upset ex wife. The Bumpster's love life had been very, very full, as Charlie had discovered previously.

There were three former wives', the Bump had told people he wished all of his 'exes lived in Texas' like that famous country western song (forgot who sang it?) instead of the OC. Their names were, Donna (married 15 years), Jean (5 years) and Jennifer (3 years). Also, there were five former 'love of his life' (temporarily anyway) ex girlfriends. Their names were; Loretta, Maggie, Icolin, Frenchie and Terri.

The Anaheim Police Department had documented copies of several hate-filled, and vicious, written communications to the Donald from all eight of them. These emails and letters, against Mr. Bump's life, appeared to make all five of these women possible perpetrators (perp's) in this subject investigation. And you know good old Charlie, what did he do next? Yes, you are correct, he made another of his famous lists. A copy is attached herewith:

DONNA

She was Bumpy's first wife with whom he had two sons. She was born in Youngstown, Ohio, but raised in LA (Los Angeles, Ca). She had a violent temper and could go from '0 to 60' in just a few seconds, she really could. The Donald still has nightmares about her, very, very scary ones, indeed.

She was upset that he did not give her more alimony money. Or, that he did not die before the divorce so that she could collect on his Million Dollar life insurance policy. A very good prospect, Charlie said to himself.

JEAN

She was short only about 5' 2", very manipulative and evil woman. She held a grudge and never forgave anybody anything, ever. She was always mad at Bump for working so many hours, even though most of his hard-earned money went to her private bank account. She did not know how to make money, but she was an expert at spending it. She really was. Charlie noted, yes, another good candidate.

JENNIFER

Shorter than Jean, only 4' 11", very stocky, and she tells people that she is a Rockin mom, whatever that means. She is a very aggressive and pushy woman, although quite street smart. She is still close friends with both Jean and Donna for some unknown reason.

She got Bump into trouble with the California State Board of Realtors, which was a good thing it turns out. She is very evil, but Charlie said that he did not see her as the criminal in this case.

LORRETTA

She was also from Ohio, and a smooth talker with a salesperson personality. She sold used cars at a dealership in the Tustin Auto Center, just off of the 5 (Santa Ana) Freeway in the OC. That was where she had met Bump and she had sold him several cars before they started dating.

She had told a co-worker, that she would like to run over the Donald with one of the cars that she had sold him. A definite possibility Charlie told Howard (at the CIA).

MAGGIE

She was from Seattle in Washington State. She loves to fish and she met Bumpy on one of those half-day charter fishing boats out of lovely Dana Point in the OC. She said recently in an email that she wishes she had thrown Bumpy overboard while they were fishing and that she wished that he had drowned. Charlie thought that she was just all talk and did not feel that she was a good prospect, at all.

ICOLIN

She was from Jamaica, in the beautiful Caribbean. She loved to dance at late night salsa clubs in LA (Los Angeles) and also the OC. She had met bumpy at an afterhours Rave in Irvine. She was a very good dancer, and he was not, but he thought he was, she said. Not a good candidate either, Charlie said.

FRENCHIE

She was born near Leon (Near Paris) France, hence her nickname, Frenchie. She had owned a bar in Munich, Germany at one time, then lived in London, England before coming to the USA 20 years ago. She met Bump at the Balboa Bay Yacht club in Newport Beach.

They both had sail boats and loved the ocean. She could not speak English very well even though she has been here for many years. She had a very quick temper and was hyper active. Move and walked and talked very fast. Charlie knew she was not well enough versed in English, nor computers to be a serious candidate in this case.

TERRI

She was very tall, little bit heavy set, but still pretty. She had five kids and she wanted Bumpy to marry her so that he would support them and also, she wanted to quit working and travel the world, on his dime, so to speak. She took their breakup very, very hard, she really did.

She worked at a software computer company in Irvine, just off of the 405 Freeway. Also, she was in the California National Guard and she was assigned to the Armory. Yes, Charlie thought, a possible suspect, indeed.

Charlie called his old buddy Howard (CIA) and told him that in the 'Love Interest' department he had four very viable suspects in the Bumpy Death Threat investigation, and they were as follows:

Donna,
Jean,
Loretta, and
Terri

Then Charlie went on to tell Howard that in the 'Disgruntled real estate client area', there were three more potential criminals, making a total of seven possible perp's. After which he listed those three, in summary fashion:

Shari,
Christine, and
Jack

After reviewing the consolidated suspect list with Howard, Howard told Charlie that he would run the 'magnificent seven' potential killers through the CIA 'Behavioral Science' section's team and sophificated software computer lab. And, after he got the results he would get back to Charlie a sap, and relay who his experts in these- type of case's and their computers, believed were the most likely guilty party/parties in this investigation into the Death Threats of Mr. Bump.

Yes, Charlie said to himself, Bumpy was a cad, philanderer, cheater, non-Christian, nonracist, not to mention an ego maniac, liar and a crook. And yet he did not deserve to be blow into 'little bits' for his past indiscretions.

In Charlie's opinion any way, and also Charlie knew that our Dios will take care of the Bumpster sooner or later, and he will visit the gates of Hades one day.

Charlie called his good buddy Howard (at the CIA) and told him that in the 'Love Interest' department he had four viable candidates in the Bumpy's death threat investigation. And, they were as follows:

DONNA

Read bad Karma waiting to happen. Like the old by Carlos Santana (with Leon Patillo) a Black Magic woman with her evil ways (also see former list for more details about her).

JEAN

A big time and world class nightmare. Vile to the core and mean-spirited woman, she truly was.

LORETTA

Usually people from the mid west are great people, but she was an exception. She was sneaky and ran around on her new husband (number 5). She would give you a great big smile and then turn right around and put a dagger in your back.

TERRI

She is not a very forgiving person and now she is a man hater, albeit, she has some good reasons, it would appear. She was at one time a sweet heart of a woman, but people do change. Some change for the better and some change for the worse. In her case, sadly to say, it was for the worse.

SHARI

A $250,000.00 financial loss is a good reason to be mad or even hate someone, a very good reason. Also, she had Motive, means (knowhow), and Opportunity to commit this heinous crime.

CHRISTINE

It was not just the $25,000.00 loss that made her despise the Bumpster. It was also the fact that he cheated on her as well as all of those nasty and unwelcome roaches (that had escaped from the Roach Hotel).

JACK

He had a very bad as well as violent temper. And, he also had the expertise to carry out this severe hate crime (See another list).

One morning at 0600 (6 am Pacific time) and 0300 (3 am Eastern time) Charlie got an encrypted text message from Howard. It stated that his experts at the CIA had determined that the most likely criminals behind the serious Death Threats to Mr. Bump, were two women working together.

Namely Donna, and Loretta. They both had the Motive, Means, and Opportunity to commit these cowardly acts. Charlie was not surprised, at their outcome, not at all.

Then Charlie got a second secure text from Howard. And it said that after the Orange County District Attorney's office completed their investigation of these two-evil woman, and IF they were not the guilty parties (as they appear to be), then Charlie should re investigate (revisit) the other five potential suspects in this case. And they were, Jean, Terri, Shari, Christine and Jack.

After reading Howard's two very crucial texts, Charlie thanked his good friend, profusely, and then said that he would keep him posted on the OC DA's investigation, and or, prosecution et al.

Yes, Charlie thought to himself, "You just solved another Mystery. You're the man." And then he thought again, is it really solved? Or could it have been another woman, or man, whom wished for Mr. Bump to be floating in the air in little pieces?

TEN

CHARLIE HAS BEEN going to the wonderfully entertaining as well as fun 'Knott's Berry Farm' since the 1960's. Also, he practically raised his two-great son's (David and Mark) there. He took them there about once a month for most of their childhoods from about 1970's to the 1980's. His kids absolutely loved the 'Farm' as did Charlie.

They saw and rode all of the attractions and each time they got a new one, they had to see it and try it out. For years, they had a Lagoon on the east side of Beach Boulevard, across the street from the main park. It had live pack mules to ride, a big white river boat, little paddle boats, and a real neat little train.

Plus, it also had the famous replica of Independence Hall in Philadelphia, Pennsylvania. A lot of the time, Charlie would just take the boys to that side of the Park, and other times he would take them into the main area on the West side of Beach Boulevard. Beach Boulevard is quite a well-known thoroughfare that runs from Whittier Boulevard in La Habra Heights, and dead ends, into the famous Huntington State Main Beach and Pier. (AKA, also known as, Surf City USA).

Charlie's secretary, Lucy Liu, got a message from Edward Heinz, the President and CEO (Chief Executive Officer) of Cedar Fair Entertainment Company. That is the corporation that purchased 'Knott's Berry Farm' from the Walter and Cordelia Knott's children. The Knott kids had inherited the very successful and quite profitable, family business in the 1990's when their parents passed away. The children had sold the Food part (which was separate from the Theme Park) to the J.M. Sm*ucker* company at the same time.

Mr. Heinz had told Lucy that someone had been sabotaging some of the rides at the family friendly berry park. He added that they have professional security guards, in uniform, on the premises, and also, they had lots and lots of plain clothes security officers all over the park.

They were dressed just like tourists and no one would suspect by looking at them that they were anything but visitors. They carried cameras, had umbrellas, big hats, theme hats, wore shorts with T-Shirts with Berry Farm characters on them, et cetera.

Mr. Heinz, added that even though he had his security personnel closely watching for the perpetrator (the perp as Charlie would call him/her) and had also hired 25 new guards, they could not figure out who the vile culprit was.

He said that Charlie's name and number had been given to him by the Anaheim Police Department as well as the Buena Park (Where the Park is located) Police Department, and also the Chief Security Officer for Disneyland (which is very close to the Berry Farm. And It is located in Anaheim). They all recommended Charlie very highly to Mr. Heinz and told him that Charlie was a retired Police Detective after 20 years with the LAPD (e.g., Los Angeles Police Department).

As soon as Lucy told Charlie about the call, he immediately told her to call Mr. Heinz back and tell him he would take the case. He would need to be named Chief of Security for the Park until the bad guy/gal was found.

Also, his fee would be $2,000.00 per diem (day) plus all expenses, and he would need one of the private hotel rooms at the Park for VIP guests that most people do not even know exist. He wanted to be close to the action and on call 24/7 until the case was solved.

In addition, he had Lucy tell Mr. Heinz that he would need the Berry Farm to also hire his three PI's (Charlie's Angels) as his back up operatives for this very dangerous assignment. He needed people he could trust completely and also people whom he could count on to 'watch his back'.

And for all Charlie knew the sociopath, or psychopath, who was causing all of the panic and worry at the Park, and very possibly future tourist's deaths, might, might just be one of the security guards, or another type of employee at the Berry Farm. Like Charlie always says, "It is better to be safe than sorry."

Before Charlie could move into his new Digs (living quarters) at the Knott's Berry Farm secret special guest rooms, he got another call from Mr. Heinz who told Charlie that the quite popular Ghost Rider Roller Coaster Ride had a serious malfunction.

Thank God that no visitors were killed, however, 20 of them had to be escorted off of the high above the ground ride by the BPFD (i.e., Buena Park Fire Department) but five of them had minor injuries.

The Knott's Security Staff said it was definitely not an accident, and then added that it was definitely an act of Sabotage. The heinous criminal had obviously just struck again. Charlie decided that he should move into his new apartment at the Park that day.

Right away, instead of next week as he had planned. He felt that he had no time to waste in finding the perp (perpetrator). Also, he did not want anyone to get killed, nor have any more visitors injured, or almost scared to death at the very friendly family Theme Park. They have a 'Knott's Scary Farm' activity at the Farm, but, that was only for Halloween and Charlie did not want it to be for real.

Thank our *Dios* (God) no one had died yet at the Berry Farm, but our man Charlie knew it was only a matter of time before these cowardly acts of Domestic Terrorism (so to speak) would result in the dearth of at least one, or quite possibly several dozens of tourists. The bad PR (Public Relations and news reports) would seriously hurt the Parks attendance and income (bottom line) as well as their long- time pristine reputation.

The Theme Park owners, Cedar Fair Entertainment Company, however, were more concerned, much more concerned, about the safety of the families who visit and love this Park, and their children as well as their parents/guardians.

Charlie and his three PI (Private Investigator) Angels started their investigation the moment their boots hit the ground at Knott's Berry Farm. Angel number one, Letty Montez started be part of the investigation by looking into the confidential employment records of all of the current (and also the recent past) security staff. All of the security guards as well as the security departments supervisors.

Angel number two, Gabby Arnez began her part by examining the employment records of all of the rest of the Parks general employees. That included the sales people, maintenance workers, housekeeping, cleaning, construction workers, set decorators, character performers, ticket sales/ takers, food court vender's, as well as all of the rest of the non-security staff.

Angel number three, Lulu Bermudez was charged with investigating the Farms sub-contractor's. That included all of the numerous gardeners, supplies/gift item delivery people, truck drivers, and also the computer software consultants (of which there were many).

Charlie had decided that he would concentrate on looking into the senior staff and also the executives at the world-famous Knott's Berry Farm. These individuals were the least likely to be the guilty party/parties, however, they had to be eliminated as the possible culprits.

Also, he planned on checking out any recently terminated officers/executives from the Park. Anyone whom had just lost a high paying job, and was disgruntled about it, would make a good suspect, a very good suspect indeed, Charlie thought to himself.

On the third day that Charlie and his *Angels* were on site at the Farm, there was another (number three) staged' accident. This time it was on the Voyage to the Iron Reef attraction. Once again, thank God, no one was killed, nor seriously hurt. There were, however, 15 children slightly injured.

Charlie said to himself out loud this time, "This has just got to stop. And it has to stop very soon before things get any worse."

Knott's Berry Farm is a 160-acre amusement park in Buena Park, California, owned by Cedar Fair Entertainment Company. Since the amusement park's acquisition by Cedar Fair, the park's annual attendance has steadily increased. The 2014 Global Attractions Attendance Report states Knott's Berry Farm is the 13th most visited theme park in North America.

The park employs approximately 10,000 seasonal and full-time employees. The park features 40 rides including roller coasters, family rides, children's rides, water rides, and historical rides, with plans to expand in the future. The park is accessible by public transportation.

The theme park sits on the site of a former berry farm established by Walter Knott, Cordelia Knott, and their family. Beginning around 1920, the Knott family sold berries, berry preserves, and pies from a roadside stand along State Route 39. In 1934, the Knott's began selling fried chicken dinners in a tea room on the property, and the Knott's built several shops and other attractions to entertain visitors.

Cordelia Knott's efforts in the Mrs. Knott's Chicken Dinner Restaurant were essential to putting Knott's Berry Farm on the map, and the ensuing crowds prompted the creation of even more tourist attractions.

In 1940, Walter Knott began constructing a replica Ghost Town on the property. Knott added several other attractions over the years and began charging admission to the attractions in 1968. In 1983, Knott's Berry Farm added Camp Snoopy, which began the park's present-day association with the Peanuts characters.

In the 1990s, following the deaths of Walter and Cordelia Knott, their children sold the family business; the theme park was sold to Cedar Fair, while the food business was sold to ConAgra Foods, which subsequently sold to J. M. Smucker. J.M. Smucker reduced the range of products but has continued to make jams, jellies and preserves. Cedar Fair has continued to expand the theme park, adding Knott's Soak City in 1999 and adding other rides to the original park.

The theme park sits on the site of a former berry farm established by Walter Knott and his family. Beginning around 1920, the Knott family sold berries, berry preserves, and pies from a roadside stand along State Route 39. In 1934, the Knott's began selling fried chicken dinners in a tea room on the property, later called "Mrs. Knott's Chicken Dinner Restaurant".

The dinners soon became a major tourist draw, and the Knott's built several shops and other attractions to entertain visitors while waiting for a seat in the restaurant. In 1940, Walter Knott began constructing a replica Ghost Town on the property, the beginning of the present-day theme park.

The idea of an amusement park really picked up in the 1950's when Walter Knott opened a "summer-long county fair". In 1968, for the first time, an admission price was required to get into the park, originally set at 25 cents. The Calico log ride was added in 1969. On April 12, 1974, Cordelia Knott died. Walter turned his attention toward political causes.

The 1970's saw a Roaring Twenties re-themed Gypsy Camp with the addition of a nostalgic traditional amusement area, Wheeler Dealer Bumper Cars and Knott's Bear-y Tales. Then there came the northward expansion of a 1920s-era Knott's Airfield themed area featuring the Cloud 9 Dance Hall, Sky Cabin/Parachute Sky Jump and Motorcycle Chase steeple chase roller coaster above the electric guided rail Gasoline Alley car ride. The expansion was inspired by the innovative new roller coaster Corkscrew.

Sky Tower was built to support two attractions, the Parachute Sky Jump (now closed) and the Sky Cabin. Parachute Sky Jump boarded one or two standing riders anticipating the thrill of the drop into baskets beneath a faux parachute canopy. From the top, eight arms supported the vertical cable tracks of wire rope which lifted the baskets.

When built, Sky Tower was the tallest structure in Orange County (a distinction briefly held by *Wind Seeker* before its relocation to *Worlds of Fun* in 2012.) The illuminated "K" in logo script atop the Sky Tower was designated a landmark which prevented Knott's plan of converting the foundation to support Wind Seeker.

Corkscrew debuted in 1975 as the first modern-day roller coaster to perform a 360-degree inverting element, twice. It was designed by Arrow Development. Corkscrew is still operating to this day but was sold and relocated in 1989 to Silverwood in Athol, Idaho. *Montezuma's Revenge* was later opened in 1978 and remains in operation at Knott's Berry Farm.

Motorcycle Chase, a modernized steeplechase rollercoaster built in 1976 by Arrow Development, featured single motorbike themed vehicles racing side-by-side, each on one of four parallel tracks, launched together. One or two riders straddled each "Indian motorcycle" attraction vehicle. The tubular steel monorail track closely followed dips and bumps in "the road" and tilted to lean riders about the curves. Gasoline Alley, an electric steel-guiderail car ride below, was built together and intimately intertwined, which enhanced ride-to-ride interaction thrill value.

Rider safety concerns of the high center of gravity coupled with the method of rider restraints caused it to be re-themed Wacky Soap Box Racers with vehicles now attached in four car trains, each car seated two riders, strapped in low (nearly straddling the track), surrounded by the close-fitting car sides, and the dips and bumps of the track were straightened flat in 1980. Motorcycle Chase/Wacky Soap Box Racers was removed 1996 for a dueling loop coaster Windjammer Surf Racers and now Xcelerator, a vertical launch coaster, takes its place.

On December 3, 1981, Walter Knott died. He was survived by his children who would continue to operate Knott's as a family business for another fourteen years. In the 1980s, Knott's built the Barn Dance featured Bobbi & Clyde as the house band. It was during the height of the "Urban Cowboy" era. The "Barn Dance" was featured in Knott's TV Commercials.

During the 1980s, Knott's met the competition in Southern California theme parks by creating a new land and building two massive attractions: 1) Kingdom of the Dinosaurs (1987) (Primeval re-theme of Knott's Bear-y Tales) and 2) Bigfoot Rapids (1988), a whitewater river rafting ride as the centerpiece of the new themed area Wild Water Wilderness.

The Boomerang roller coaster replaced the Corkscrew in 1990 with a lift shuttle train passing to and fro through a cobra roll and a vertical loop for six inversions each trip. Mystery Lodge (1994), inspired by General Motors "Spirit Lodge" pavilion, was a live show augmented with Peppers Ghost and other special effects, which was among the most popular exhibits at Expo 86 in Vancouver, British Columbia, Canada, which was produced by Bob Rogers of BRC Imagination Arts and created with the assistance of the Kwagulth Native reserve in Alert Bay, British Columbia.

Mystery Lodge recreates a quiet summer night in the village of Alert Bay, British Columbia then guests "move inside" the longhouse and listen to the storyteller weave a tale of the importance of family from the smoke of the bonfire. The Jaguar! was opened June 17, 1995, to add another roller coaster to the mix of Fiesta Village alongside Montezuma's Revenge.

New Owners: In the 1990s, after Walter and Cordelia died, their children decided to sell off their businesses. In the late 1990s Cedar Fair acquired the Buena Park Hotel at the corner of Grand Ave. and Crescent. It was then brought up to Radisson Standards and branded Radisson Resort Hotel as a franchise. In 2004, the park renamed the Radisson Resort Hotel the Knott's Berry Farm Resort Hotel. In 1995, the Knott family sold the food specialty business to ConAgra Foods, which later re-sold the brand to The J.M. Smucker Company in 2008.

In 1997, the Knott family sold the amusement park operations to Cedar Fair Entertainment Company. Initially, the Knott's were given an opportunity to sell the park to The Walt Disney Company. The park would have been amalgamated into the Disneyland Resort and converted into Disney's America, which had previously failed to be built near Washington, D.C. The Knott's refused to sell the park to Disney out of fear most of what Walter Knott had built would be eliminated.

Since being acquired by Cedar Fair, the park has seen an aggressive shift towards thrill rides, with the construction of a number of large roller coasters and the addition of a high-performance Shoot-the-Chutes ride Perilous Plunge.

Perilous Plunge had the record of being the tallest and steepest water ride in the world until September 2012 when Knott's Berry Farm closed and demolished the water attraction. Also, in 2013, Knott's Berry Farm announced that the most popular ride at the park, the Timber Mountain Log Ride, would be closed for a major 5 month refurbishment.

On May 25, 2013, Knott's Berry Farm added three new family rides which replaced the spot of Perilous Plunge. They include: Coast Rider (wild mouse roller coaster), Pacific Scrambler (scrambler ride) and Surfside Gilders. All three of the rides added to the theme of the Boardwalk.

The old bridge which connected the exit of Perilous Plunge and the boardwalk is now used as the entrance to Surfside Gilders and Pacific Scrambler. The Boomerang roller coaster was also repainted to a lime-green color as part of the Boardwalk expansion.

On May 29, 2013, Knott's Timber Mountain Log Ride reopened after a five-month refurbishment. The ride was updated with new animations and new scenes. Notable was the addition of new pine trees which were planted outside the ride's mountain. The log's front icons also received new updated icons as part of the major refurbishment.

On September 2, 2013, Knott's Berry Farm announced that Wind seeker would be closed and removed from the park. After the ride was closed by Cedar Fair for safety inspection, the ride was never cleared to operate. The ride was removed and sent to Worlds of Fun for the 2014 season.

On November 22, 2013, Knott's Berry Farm made a major announcement for the 2014 operating season. The park announced that the famous and historical ride, the Calico Mine Ride, would be closed for a major 6-month refurbishment beginning in January 2014.

The major refurbishment is occurring due to the successful transformation of the 5-month refurbishment of the Timber Mountain Log Ride. Camp Snoopy will also receive an improved transformation as it is approaching its 30th anniversary. The park announced Camp Snoopy would receive a makeover with new rides.

Annual Park Events: The park's annual Knott's Scary Farm has drawn crowds since 1973. The idea for this event was presented at one of the regularly scheduled round table meetings for managers by Patricia Pawson.

Several attractions are decorated for the event including the Timber Mountain Log Ride and Calico Mine Train and there are 13 mazes of various themes. Elvira (actress Cassandra Peterson) was introduced into the Halloween Event in 1982 and was prominently featured in many Halloween Haunt events until 2001.

According to postings on her My Space page, Cassandra was released from her contract by the park's new owners due to their wanting a more family friendly appeal, although she returned for one night in 2012 for the 40th anniversary of the event. During the month of October, Knott's Scary Farm generates half the revenue for Knott's Berry Farm's fiscal year.

Season of Screams is a DVD produced by an independent company which traces the beginnings of Halloween Haunt and the story behind how it all got started back in 1973. Season of Screams also highlights recent Halloween Haunts.

Winter Coaster Solace is an event that takes place every year when roller coaster enthusiasts can come before the park opens and stay after the park closes to ride the rides and eat at the Chicken Dinner Restaurant. It is intended to provide "solace" to visitors from other parts of the country where theme parks and roller coasters are seasonal, not year-round operations like the Southern California parks. Knott's Berry Farm also used to give attendees behind the scenes tours of the rides.

Every year since 1991, Knott's has offered free admission to veterans and their families during the month of November. Though this was originally started as a tribute to returning Gulf War veterans, they subsequently expanded it to include all veterans and have run it every year since.

A Christmas event known as "Knott's Merry Farm" also happens annually. Praise (festival) has been a Christian themed celebration presented many years as a mix-in special event of music and comedy on New Year's Eve.

Charlie loves all four of the Knott's Berry Farm's themed areas in the Farm. He truly does. Fiesta Village is great Latino flavored food and fun area, and the Boardwalk has lots of newer rides and attractions. And his kids absolutely loved Camp Snoopy as they were growing up, just as the little kids do even today 30 years later.

Charlie says that he could spend days, and days, going to the different themed areas and never get tired of them or the Park nor the great chicken, food and snacks, of course. He told his Angels that he had not been there for several years since his boys are all grown up now, and are both cop's in the OC.

And after they resolved this important very serious Sabotage investigation, he was going to come back and visit every month from now on. He told them that he was going to get one of their neat-season passes and suggested that they get one as well.

ELEVEN

SPEAKING OF GHOST Town, Charlie just loves Ghost Town, he truly does. He always loved to walk up and down the old looking dirt streets, look into the old general store, the saloon, the smith shop, the bottle house, the knife shop, and naturally the old jail for the bad cowboys back in the day.

Charlie would sit on the old wooden benches and in his little mind, be back in the olden days when things were so much simpler and not to mention there were fewer criminals roaming about than there are in today's crazy society.

Then while Charlie relaxed and reflected about the good ole days long gone, he read some more important information about the history of the fabulous Ghost Town at one of his all -time favorite places, 'Knott's Berry Farm.'

Craftsmen in Ghost Town demonstrate the arts of the blacksmith, woodcarver, glass-blower, sign cutter and spinner. Demonstrations of narrow gauge railroading and farm equipment hobbyists accompany additional merchant stalls of cottage-craft fairs seasonally at discounted admission which is restricted to Ghost Town only.

Charlie loves the Western Trails Museum, relocated between the candy store (he loves the candy store as well, naturally) and the General Store to accommodate Bigfoot Rapids, still features historical western artifacts large and small, from a hand powered horse-drawn fire engine to miniature replica of a borax hauling "Twenty Mule Team" and utensils necessary to survive the prairie and wilderness.

The Ghost Town area has a few other notable attractions. The Bird Cage Theatre only hosts two seasonal entertainments – during "Knott's

Merry Farm" there are two small productions of "The Gift of the Magi" and "A Christmas Carol" and a Halloween Haunt thrill show.

The Calico Stage, a large open-air stage in Calico Square, hosts a variety of shows and acts, big and small, from those of elementary school students, like Gallagher, a local band and the summer-spectacular All Wheels Extreme stunt show featuring youthful performers demonstrating aerial tricks with acrobatics, trampolines, and riding ramps with skates, scooters, skateboards, and freestyle bikes to popular music.

Calico Saloon recreates the revelry of music, singing and dancing, with Cameo Kate hosting a variety of acts. Jersey Lily, a Judge Roy Bean's combination courthouse/saloon, offers certified comical "genuine illegal hitchin'" alongside pickles, candy, and sports/soft drinks.

Many parts of Ghost Town are forever lost to progress. The conversion of the Silver Dollar Saloon to a shooting gallery, Hunters Paradise shooting gallery to Panda Express and the original Berry Stand, moved several times with its last location now occupied by the Silver Bullet station.

What is left of Ghost Town today was based on Calico ghost town and other real ghost towns in the Western United States such as Prescott, Arizona. Walter Knott inherited his uncle's silver mill and land, then bought more of the actual Calico ghost town in 1951 and developed it. In 1966, he donated that property to the corporate-municipal County of San Bernardino which then made the town of Calico, California into a public historic park, for which it charged an entrance/parking fee.

The Boardwalk: Originally themed as Gypsy Camp, and later re-themed to the "Roaring '20s", "Knott's Airfield", then "The Boardwalk", this area is home to the most of Knott's major thrill rides.

Perilous Plunge was known as one of Knott's major thrill rides. The boardwalk reopened after a year transformation with two flat rides and a new family roller coaster taking the spot of Perilous Plunge. The Boomerang roller coaster also got repainted with a new vibrant green and yellow color scheme.

The world's largest Johnny Rockets restaurant franchise is located at Knott's Boardwalk, featuring over 5,900 square feet of indoor dining space for more than 260 guests.

Knott's Berry Farm also built the Mall of America's indoor theme park, which itself was originally called Camp Snoopy. (In fact, Charles M. Schulz hailed from St. Paul). Today the park is no longer affiliated with Knott's or Cedar Fair and is now called Nickelodeon Universe.

On November 22, 2013, Knott's Berry Farm announced major improvements in the area of Camp Snoopy. Camp Snoopy will receive a makeover as the section is approaching its 30th anniversary. In summer 2014, Knott's Berry Farm will open up new rides in Camp Snoopy.

The 2 ft narrow gauge Grand Sierra Scenic Railroad takes guests on a four-minute train ride through the reflection lake. The ride was made shorter with the construction of Silver Bullet.

Located next to the Bottle House in Ghost Town, Indian Trails is a small area sandwiched between Camp Snoopy, Ghost Town, and Fiesta Village, showcasing Native American art, crafts and dance. One ride is located in this area. It is called Butterfield Stagecoach which is a family ride where an actual stagecoach takes guests on a circular ride through Fiesta Village and Camp Snoopy. It is one of the original rides at the park. The ride was developed directly by the park and it opened in 1949.

Many of the popular original attractions are outside the gates of the current day theme park along Grand Ave. at the California Marketplace, mostly things which would no longer be considered interesting to today's audience, or things which were merely there for decoration. Near the restrooms behind Berry Place are the waterfall overshooting the water wheel and historic gristmill grindstone, a replica of George Washington's Mount Vernon estate fireplace hearth, and what remains of the visible beehive.

Some attractions still exist, but have been incorporated into backstage areas, such as the Rock Garden, now an employee smoking area. Other attractions have been removed, such as the historic volcano, and the cross-section of giant sequoia with age rings denoting historic events such as Christopher Columbus visiting America.

ATTRACTION/CAPITAL TIMELINE
1920: Ten acres of berry farm land leased by Walter and Cordelia Knott
1927: Ten leased acres of berry farm purchased, named Knott's Berry Place.
1929: Ten more acres purchased

After three days of deep undercover investigation which lasted up to 12 hours a day, Charlie texted his three Angels and asked them to meet him at the old and quite famous 'Bird Cage Theater' (Saloon). It is located in the oldest part of the farm, the Ghost Town area of the Theme Park.

He wanted to get an update on who his very efficient PI's felt might be viable suspects in the Sabotage case. They all had some great Berry juice as well as old time Sarsaparillas.

Letty went first, she stated that a senior security guard named Gerald 'Jerry' Gunhoffer, was recently demoted from his quite high paying position at the Farm. It was discovered that he was involved (i.e. affair) with a female security staff member, and that they were both married. Also, it was alleged, but not proven, that he had several other inappropriate relationships with other female employees in the past. Some of these relationships going back several years it appeared.

After Gunhoffer's demotion his wife of 20 years found out about his affairs, and all, and took his three kids, left him and immediately filed for divorce. Jerry was very upset to say the least about this great loss and felt that it was all the Knott's Berry Farm's fault, and not his own *'carnal* sins'. Yes, very good suspect Charlie told Letty, and added good job.

Gabby went second and shared that a maintenance worker named Donald 'Don' Lowly, who had worked on all of the rides at the Theme Park, was just put on probation for showing up for work while High on drugs. He had been warned before, and also sent to drug counseling at the company's expense.

Don had told friends that he would get even for the Farm saying that he was a druggie and ruining his good reputation with his maintenance trade union. Again, Charlie added, good prospect for our perp, a very good one indeed.

Lulu went after Gabby, and third to speak. After another sarsaparilla, and berry drink for all, she said that she had found out that a regular daily delivery truck driver (but not a Farm employee) named Gordon 'Gordy' Browne, was caught trying to sell Knock-Off goods (cheaply made in Hong Kong) to some of the souvenir shops at the Park. Knott's Berry Farm has always carried only good quality items in their shops.

The security staff caught him but could not fire him since he was not a Park employee. They did report him and got him into a lot of trouble with his delivery company employer, but he was able to keep his job. Charlie nodded his head, "Yes, another possible candidate."

Charlie spoke last, he said that he was very pleased with their investigative work in such a short amount of time. He then added that he had found a good suspect as well. A man named Frank 'Frankie' Abbott, whom had previously been an Executive VP (Vice President) in charge of the Sales and Marketing Department at the Park.

Abbott had been fired (terminated with cause) last year for embezzling Two Million dollars from the Berry Farm's investment money market account. He was a very trusted and long-time officer at the Park, therefore, no one suspected him and he was able to steal small amounts of money and no one noticed a few thousand dollars at a time.

After all the Farm brought in Millions of dollars every month and it was hard to tract smaller transactions. Not even the company in- house CPA's (Certified Public Accountants) spotted the theft.

Since he was in sales, Abbott had the 'gift of gab' so to speak and was able to pull off his dastardly deed without being caught, at least for some time anyway. He made just one small mistake, and as Charlie always says, "Criminals always make a mistake, sooner or later, they always do.

And you can take that to the Bank." His mistake was to pay cash for his new little twin-engine Airplane, which he kept at the John Wayne Airport in Newport Beach. He had paid $750,000.00 cash for the nice new 6 passenger plane and did not think that anyone would notice.

He had paid cash because he did not want to monthly payments as they would show up on his bank statement. His wife and his boss at the Park often looked at his statement.

Then an external CPA and Auditor for one of the big national accounting firms, that the Park uses, noticed the *missing* cash and started a secret in-house investigation. The results stunned all of the executives at the Farm.

Then, Charlie told his Angels, "Great job, I think that we are making very good progress on our *Sabotage* case. Now let's go over to the world famous (Cornelia) Knott's Berry Farm Chicken Dinner Restaurant."

Charlie has been eating at this Restaurant for decades with his two sons and friends. Best chicken in California according to Charlie. People from all over the state, and also the USA, come to the Park just for their dinners.

Then, after Charlie, and his three Angels, had fed their faces to the max, he went back to his room with a list of all of these new suspects, four in all, and ponder which one is the most likely perp, guilty party, in this case.

Also, he wanted to dwell on the possibility that there could be, just possibly, some other criminals who were involved in these heinous acts of Sabotage.

Then sleep came upon our man Charlie, and as he slipped into never, never land, with heavy *old* eyes, he said to himself, "Charlie, that's all you can do for today. Better get some shut eye, Tomorrow is another day, and if you are lucky, real lucky, you might just catch a bad guy tomorrow, Lord willing and the creek don't rise, like John 'Duke' Wayne used to say."

TWELVE

CHARLIE WANTED TO do some more traveling down *Nostalgia Lane*, therefore, he surfed (searched the internet as it were) and wished that he was on his own long board surfing the Huntington State Beach Pier right now. He had already found lots of quite interesting and some unknown information of the Pioneer Surfer Band, "The Beach Boys." The information that he found he told us about earlier as you may recall.

The famous beach is located right where Highway 39 (Beach Boulevard dead ends into the lovely Pacific Coast Highway in Surf City USA). Well soon, Charlie told himself, "real soon." Charlie loves to just hand out at that fabulous beach and watch the lovely young women play Volley Ball in their tinny weenie little bikini's. Women's beach Volley Ball is *Charlie's* favorite sport, as I am sure all of you men will understand.

Herewith he lists a few of the wonderful and pioneering Surfer Bands that he remembered as young hippy surfer 'back in the day'.

JAN AND DEAN

Jan and Dean were an American rock and roll duo consisting of William Jan Berry (April 3, 1941 – March 26, 2004) and Dean Ormsby Torrence (born March 10, 1940). In the early 1960s, they were pioneers of the California Sound and vocal surf music styles popularized by the Beach Boys. Among their most successful songs was "Surf City", which topped US record charts in 1963, the first surf song to do so. Their other charting singles were "Drag City" (1963), "The Little Old Lady from Pasadena" (1964), and "Dead Man's Curve" (1964); the last of which was inducted into the Grammy Hall of Fame in 2008.

In 1972, Torrence won the Grammy Award for Best Album Cover

for the psychedelic rock band Pollution's first eponymous 1971 album, and was nominated three other times in the same category for albums of the Nitty Gritty Dirt Band. In 2013, Torrence's design contribution of the Surf City All-stars "In Concert" CD was named a Silver Award of Distinction at the Communicator Awards competition.

William 'Jan' Berry (born in Los Angeles, California April 3, 1941; died March 26, 2004), was the son of Clara Lorentze Mustad Berry (born September 2, 1919 in Bergen, Norway; died July 9, 2009) and aeronautical engineer William L. Berry (born December 7, 1909, in the Bronx, NY; died December 19, 2004, in Camarillo, California), Berry had been project manager of the "Spruce Goose" and flew on its only flight with Howard Hughes.

Dean Ormsby Torrence (born Los Angeles, California March 10, 1940), is the son of Natalie Ormsby Torrence (born April 10, 1911, in California; died August 10, 2008, in Los Angeles, California) and Maurice Dean Torrence (born December 5, 1907, in South Dakota; died November 16, 1997, in Los Angeles, California), a graduate of Stanford University, who was a sales manager at the Wilshire Oil Company.

1957–1959: formation: Berry and Torrence, both born in Los Angeles, California, met while students at Emerson Junior High School in Westwood, Los Angeles, and both were on the school's football team. By 1957, they were students in the Vagabond Class of 1958 at the nearby University High School, where again they were on the school's football team, the Warriors.

Berry and Torrence had adjoining lockers, and after football practice, they began harmonizing together in the showers with several other football players, including future actor James Brolin.

THE BARONS

In order to enter at a talent competition at University High School, Berry and Torrence helped form a doo-wop group known as "The Barons" (named after their high school's Hi-Y club, of which they were members), which comprised fellow University High students William "Chuck" Steele (lead singer).

Arnold P. "Arnie" Ginsburg (born November 19, 1939; 1st tenor), Wallace S. "Wally" Yagi (born July 20, 1940; 2nd tenor), John 'Sagi" Seligman (2nd tenor), with Berry singing bass, and Torrence providing falsetto. During its short duration Sandy Nelson, Torrence's neighbor, played drums, and future Beach Boy, Bruce Johnston, occasionally sang and played piano.

The Barons rehearsed for hours in the garage of Berry's parents' home at 1111 Linda Flora Drive, Bel Air, where Berry's father provided an upright piano and two two-track Ampex reel-to-reel tape recorders. During primitive recording sessions in the garage, Berry served as producer and arranger, and experimented with multi-part vocal arrangements (five years before he started working professionally with Brian Wilson)

In 1958, the Barons performed to popular acclaim at the talent competition at University High School, covering contemporary hits like "Get a Job", "Rock and Roll is Here to Stay", and "Short Shorts". However, after the contest various members of the Barons drifted away, leaving only Berry and Torrence, who tried to write their own songs.

JAN & ARNIE

After being inspired by a poster featuring a local, Hollywood burlesque performer, Virginia Lee Hicks, who was then performing as Jennie Lee, the "Bazoom Girl", at the New Follies Burlesque at 548 S. Main St, Los Angeles, Ginsburg wrote a tribute song, "Jennie Lee", that he brought to Berry and Torrence. Berry adapted the Civil War tune "Aura Lea" and arranged the harmonies.

After weeks of practice, Berry, Ginsburg, and Torrence planned to record a demo recording in Berry's garage, but Torrence was conscripted into the United States Army Reserve forcing Berry and Ginsburg to record "Jennie Lee" without Torrence, with Berry's friend and fellow University High student Donald J. Altfeld (born March 18, 1940, in Los Angeles, California) "belting out the rhythm on a children's metal high chair".

The next day Berry took their recording to Radio Recorders, a small Hollywood recording studio, to have it transferred to an acetate disc. Joe Lubin, Vice President and Head of A & R of Doris Day and Martin

Melcher's Arwin Records, was impressed and offered to add instruments and to release it through Arwin. In March 1958, the fathers of Berry and Ginsburg signed contracts authorizing Lubin to produce, arrange, and manage their sons.

Berry and Ginsburg, now christened "Jan & Arnie", re-recorded their vocals on a professional recording system. Produced by Lubin, "Jennie Lee" (Arwin 108), backed with "Gotta Get a Date" (credited to Ginsburg, Berry & Lubin), became a surprise commercial success.

According to Berry's biographer Mark A. Moore, "The song (with backing vocals, plus additional instruments added by the Ernie Freeman combo) had a raucous R&B flavor, with a bouncing bomp-bomp vocal hook that would become a signature from Jan on future recordings." Distributed by Dot Records, "Jennie Lee" was released in mid-April, entered the charts on May 10, 1958, the same day they appeared on ABC's Dick Clark Show.

"Jennie Lee" peaked at No. 3 on the Cash Box charts on June 21, 1958, No. 4 on the R&B charts, and No. 8 on the Billboard charts on June 30, 1958. Billy Ward and his Dominoes's R&B cover of "Jennie Lee" reached No. 55 in the Pop charts in June 1958, while other cover versions including that of Moon Mullican (Coral 9-61994) and Bobby Phillips & the Toppers (Tops 45-R422-49), released in 1958 failed to chart.

In July 1958, Jan & Arnie released their second single, "Gas Money" backed with "Bonnie Lou" (Arwin 111), both written by Berry, Ginsburg, and Altfeld. Like "Jennie Lee", "Gas Money" contained a few elements of what would later become surf music. It entered the Billboard charts on August 24, 1958 and peaked at No. 81 a week later.

With Sheb Wooley, the Champs, Link Wray and his Ray Men, Frankie Avalon, the Kalin Twins, and Dicky Doo & the Don'ts, Jan & Arnie were a featured act on the Summer Dance Party that toured the US East Coast, including Pennsylvania, Massachusetts and Connecticut in July 1958. By the end of the month, they traveled to Manhattan to appear on ABC's Dick Clark Show.

On August 24, 1958, Jan & Arnie played in a live show hosted by Dick Clark that featured Bobby Darin, the Champs, Sheb Wooley, the

Blossoms, the Six Teens, Jerry Wallace, Jack Jones, Rod McKuen and the Ernie Freeman Orchestra in front of nearly 12,000 fans at the first rock-n-roll show ever held at the Hollywood Bowl.

By September 6, 1958, Jan & Arnie's third and final single, "The Beat That Can't Be Beat" backed with "I Love Linda" (Arwin 113), again composed by the Berry, Ginsburg and Altfeld team, was released. However, this single failed to chart, due in part to a lack of distribution. On October 19, 1958 Jan & Arnie performed "The Beat That Can't Be Beat" on CBS's *Jack Benny Show.*

Arnie Ginsburg recorded a one-off single with a band named the Rituals on the Arwin label. The single, Girl in Zanzibar b/w Guitarro, released on vinyl in January 1959, preceding Jan and Deans first single Baby Talk, released in May 1959. Other than Arnie, the single featured; Ritchie Podolor on guitar, Sandy Nelson on drums, Bruce Johnson on piano, Dave Shostac on sax, Harper Cosby on bass and Mike Deasy on guitar. It is unclear if the actual single was released for the general public but there are several promotional copies pressed to vinyl in existence.

By the end of the year, when Torrence had completed his six-month stint at Fort Ord, Ginsburg had become disenchanted with the music business. Ginsburg enrolled in the School of Architecture and Design at the University of Southern California, and graduated in the field of product design in 1966. After graduation Ginsburg worked for several noted Los Angeles architects, among them Charles Eames,. and in December 1973 he was granted a U.S. Patent for a table he designed.

Arnie Ginsburg moved to Santa Barbara, California, in 1975, where he worked as an architectural designer, designing the innovative Ginsburg House. In September 1976 Ginsburg and Michael W. O'Neill were granted a patent for a portable batting cage.

1959–1962: early records: After Torrence returned from a six-month compulsory stint in the US Army Reserve, Berry and Torrence began to make music as "Jan and Dean." With the help of record producers Herb Alpert and Lou Adler, Jan and Dean scored a No. 10 hit with "Baby Talk" (1959), (which was incorrectly labeled as Jan & Arnie when it initially was released), their first song to contain a few of the soon-to-be-famous elements that became associated with surf music (close vocal harmonies, selective use of major and minor chords, falsetto doo-wop singing), then scored a series of hits over the next couple of years.

Playing local venues, they met and performed with the Beach Boys, and discovered the appeal of the latter's "surf sound". By this time Berry was co-writing, arranging, and producing all of Jan and Dean's original material. Berry signed a series of contracts with Screen Gems to write and produce music for Jan and Dean, as well as other artists such as Judy & Jill (Berry's girlfriend, Jill Gibson, and Dean Torrence's girlfriend, Judy Lovejoy), the Matadors and Pixie (a young female solo singer).

During this time Berry co-wrote, and/or arranged and produced songs for artists outside of Jan and Dean, including the Angels ("I Adore Him", Top 30), the Gents, the Matadors (Sinners), Judy & Jill, Pixie (un-released), Jill Gibson, Shelley Fabares, Deane Hawley, the Rip Chords ("Three Window Coupe", Top 30), and Johnny Crawford, among others.

Unlike most other rock 'n roll acts of the period, Jan and Dean did not give music their full-time attention. Jan and Dean were college students, maintaining their studies while writing and recording music and making public appearances on the side.

Torrence majored in advertising design in the school of architecture at USC, where he also was a member of the Phi Sigma Kappa fraternity. Berry took science and music classes at UCLA, became a member of Phi Gamma Delta fraternity, and entered the California College of Medicine (now the UC Irvine School of Medicine) in 1963. By 1966, Berry had completed two years of medical school.

Jan and Dean reached their commercial peak in 1963 and 1964, after they met Brian Wilson. The duo scored an impressive sixteen Top 40 hits on the *Billboard* and *Cash Box* magazine charts, with a total of twenty-six chart hits over an eight-year period (1958–1966). Jan and Brian Wilson collaborated on roughly a dozen hits and album cuts for Jan and Dean, including the number one national hit "Surf City", written by Brian Wilson, in 1963. Subsequent top 10 hits included "Drag City" (#10, 1964), the eerily portentous "Dead Man's Curve" (#8, 1964), and "The Little Old Lady from Pasadena" (#3, 1964).

In 1964, at the height of their fame, Jan and Dean hosted and performed at *The T.A.M.I. Show*, a historic concert film directed by Steve Binder. The film also featured such acts as *the Rolling Stones, Chuck Berry, Gerry & the Pacemakers, James Brown*, Billy J. Kramer & the Dakotas, Marvin Gaye, the Supremes, Lesley Gore, Smokey Robinson & the Miracles and the Beach Boys. Also in 1964, the duo performed the title track for the Columbia Pictures film *Ride the Wild Surf*, starring Fabian Forte, Tab Hunter, Peter Brown, Shelley Fabares, and Barbara Eden.

The song, penned by Jan Berry, Brian Wilson and Roger Christian, was a Top 20 national hit. The pair were also to have appeared in the film, but their roles were cut following their friendship with Barry Keenan, who had engineered the *Frank Sinatra Jr. kidnapping*.

Jan and Dean also filmed two unreleased television pilots: *Surf Scene* in 1963 and *On the Run* in 1966. Their feature film for *Paramount Pictures Easy Come, Easy Go* was canceled when Berry, as well as the film's director and other crew members, were seriously injured in a railroad accident while shooting the film in *Chatsworth, California*, in August 1965.

After the surfing craze, Jan and Dean scored two Top-30 hits in 1965: "You Really Know How to Hurt a Guy" and "I Found a Girl"—the latter from the album *Folk 'n Roll*. During this period, they also began to experiment with cutting-edge comedy concepts such as the original (unreleased) *Filet of Soul* and *Jan & Dean Meet Batman*. The former's album cover shows Berry with his leg in a cast as a result of the accident while filming *Easy Come, Easy Go*.

On April 12, 1966, Berry received severe head injuries in an automobile accident on Whittier Drive, just a short distance from Dead Man's Curve in Beverly Hills, California, two years after the song had become a hit. He was on his way to a business meeting when he crashed his Corvette into a parked truck on Whittier Drive, near the intersection of Sunset Boulevard, in Beverly Hills.

He also had separated from his girlfriend of seven years, singer-artist Jill Gibson, later a member of the Mamas & the Papas for a short time, who also had co-written several songs with him. Berry was in a coma for nearly two months; he awoke on the morning of June 16, 1966.

Berry traveled a long and difficult road toward recovery from brain damage and partial paralysis. He had minimal use of his right arm and had to learn to write with his left hand. Doctors said he would never walk again, but he refused to give up, and ultimately succeeded. Torrence stood by his partner, maintaining their presence in the music industry, and keeping open the possibility that they would perform together again.

In Berry's absence Torrence released several singles on the J&D Record Co. label and recorded *Save for a Rainy Day* in 1966, a concept album featuring all rain-themed songs. Torrence posed with Berry's brother Ken for the album cover photos. Columbia Records released one single from the project ("Yellow Balloon") as did the song's writer, Gary Zekley, with the Yellow Balloon, but with legal wrangles scuttling Torrence's Columbia deal and Berry's disapproval of the project, *Save for a Rainy Day* remained a self-released album on the J&D Record Co. label (JD-101).

Besides his studio work, Torrence became a graphic artist, starting his own company, Kittyhawk Graphics, and designing and creating album covers and logos for other musicians and recording artists, including Harry Nilsson, Steve Martin, the Nitty Gritty Dirt Band, Dennis Wilson, Bruce Johnston, the Beach Boys, Diana Ross and the Supremes, Linda Ronstadt, Canned Heat, the Ventures and many others. Torrence (with Gene Brownell) won a Grammy Award for "Album Cover of the Year", for the group Pollution in 1973.

Berry returned to the studio in April 1967, almost one year to the day after his accident. Working with collaborators, he began writing and producing music again. In December 1967, Jan and Dean signed an agreement with Warner Bros. Records. Warner issued three singles under the name "Jan and Dean," but a 1968 Berry-produced album for Warner Bros., the psychedelic *Carnival of Sound*, remained unreleased until February 2010, when Rhino Records' "Handmade" label put out CD and vinyl compilations of all tracks recorded for *Carnival*, along with various outtakes and remixes from the project.

In 1971 Jan & Dean released the album *Jan & Dean Anthology Album* under the label United Artists Records. The album included many of their top hits, starting with 1958's "Jennie Lee" and ending with 1968's "Vegetables".

Berry began to sing again in the early 1970s, and he arranged and produced a number of singles (both solo and as Jan & Dean) between 1972 and 1978 on the Ode and A&M labels, facilitated by friend and former manager *Lou Adler*. Berry also toured with his Aloha band, while Dean began performing with a band called Papa Doo Run Run.

In 1973, Jan and Dean made an appearance at the Hollywood Palladium, as part of Jim Pewter's "Surfer's Stomp" reunion, in which the duo attempted to lip sync "Surf City," but the backing track failed, and they were booed off stage. The duo's first live performance after Berry's accident occurred at the *Palomino* Nightclub in *North* Hollywood on June 5, 1976, ten years after the accident, as guests of Disneyland regulars Papa Doo Run Run.

Their first actual multi-song concert billed as Jan and Dean took place in 1978 in New York City at the Palladium as part of the Murray the K Brooklyn Fox Reunion Show. This was followed by a handful of East Coast shows as guests of their longtime friends the Beach Boys.

Four nationwide J & D headlining tours followed through 1980. Jan was still suffering the effects of his 1966 accident, with partial paralysis and aphasia. He had a noticeable limp and his right arm was useless. In addition, his speech was slowed down a bit to keep up with his still almost genius IQ.

On February 3, 1978, CBS aired a made-for-TV film about the duo titled *Deadman's Curve*. The biopic starred Richard Hatch as Jan Berry and Bruce Davison as Dean Torrence, with cameo appearances by Dick Clark, Wolfman Jack, Mike Love of the Beach Boys, and Bruce Johnston (who at that time was temporarily out of the Beach Boys), as well as Berry himself.

Near the end of the film he can be seen sitting in the audience, watching "himself" (Richard Hatch) perform onstage. The part of Jan & Dean's band was played by Papa Doo Run Run, which included Mark Ward and Jim Armstrong, who went on to form Jan & Dean and the Bel-Air Bandits.

Johnston and Berry had known each other since high school and had played music together in Berry's garage in Bel Air—long before Jan & Dean or the Beach Boys were formed. Following the release of the film, the duo made steps toward an official comeback that year, including touring with the Beach Boys, and performing with Papa Doo Run Run at Cupertino High School.

In the early 1980s, Papa Doo Run Run left to explore other performance and recording ventures. Berry struggled to overcome drug addiction. In 1979, Jan had performed over 100 concerts of Jan and Dean songs with another front man from Hawaii, Randy Ruff. Torrence also toured briefly as "Mike & Dean," with Mike Love of the Beach Boys. Later, the duo reunited for good. In "Phase II" of their career, Dean led the touring operation. In 1986, Berry helped establish the Jan Berry Center for the Brain Injured in Downey, California. Though he only made a partial recovery, Berry remained a high-profile example for patients with traumatic brain injury.

Jan and Dean continued to tour on their own throughout the 1980s, 1990s, and into the new millennium—with 1960s nostalgia providing them with a ready audience, headlining oldies shows throughout North America. Noted Chicago Tribune columnist Bob Greene penned a 2008 book, *When We Get to Surf City: A Journey Through America in Pursuit of Rock and Roll, Friendship, and Dreams*, detailing his occasional appearances with Jan & Dean's touring band throughout the 1990s and early 2000s.

Sundazed Records reissued Torrence's *Save for a Rainy Day* in 1996 in CD and vinyl formats, as well as the collector's vinyl 45" companion EP, "Sounds for A Rainy Day," featuring four instrumental versions of the album's tracks.

Between the 1970s and the early 2000s, Torrence issued a number of re-recordings of classic Jan and Dean and Beach Boys hits. A double album titled *One Summer Night / Live* was issued by Rhino Records in 1982. Torrence released the album *Silver Summer* with the help of Mike Love in 1985 for Jan & Dean's 25th anniversary. *Silver Summer* was officially released as a Jan & Dean album, but falsely gives credit to Berry as co-producer and singer. Berry did not partake in the album.

Torrence participated with Berry on *Port to Paradise*, released as a cassette on the J&D Records label in 1986. In 1997, after many years of hard work, Berry released a solo album called *Second Wave* on One Way Records. June 11, 2002, Torrence released a solo album titled, *Anthology:*

Legendary Masked Surfer Unmasked.

On August 31, 1991, Berry married Gertie Filip at the Stardust Convention Centre in *Las Vegas, Nevada*. Torrence was Berry's best man at the wedding.

Jan and Dean's long career together ended with Jan Berry's death on March 26, 2004, after he suffered a seizure eight day before his 63rd birthday. Berry was an organ donor, and his body was cremated. On April 18, 2004, a "Celebration of Life" was held in Berry's memory at the Roxy Theatre on the Sunset Strip in West Hollywood, California. Attendees included Torrence, Lou Adler, Jill Gibson, and Nancy Sinatra, along with many family members, friends, and musicians associated with Jan and Dean and the Beach Boys, including the original members of Papa Doo Run Run.

In February 2010, the legendary unreleased Jan & Dean album "Carnival of Sound" was released on the Rhino Handmade label. The album cover was designed by Torrence. Along with the CD, there is a limited (to 1500 copies) edition which includes a 10-track LP. The album was released in Europe in April 2010 in its original US form.

In 2012, Torrence reunited with Bruce Davison, who portrayed him in the 1978 film "Deadman's Curve," to perform with the Bamboo Trading Company on their *From Kitty Hawk To Surf City* album. The songs were "Shrewd Awakening" and "Tonga Hut", which was featured on the film *Return of the Killer Shrews*, a sequel to the 1959 film *The Killer Shrews* and also "Tweet (Don't Talk Anymore)", "Drinkin' In the Sunshine", and "Star Of The Beach". The album also features Dean's two daughters, Jillian and Katie Torrence. Torrence and his two daughters were featured in the music video of "Shrewd Awakening".

Torrence now tours occasionally with the Surf City All-Stars. He serves as a spokesman for the City of Huntington Beach, California, which, thanks in-part to his efforts, is nationally recognized as "Surf City USA." Dean's website, Jan & Dean, features—among other things—rare images, a complete Jan & Dean discography, a biography, and a timeline of his career with cohort Jan Berry. He currently resides in Huntington Beach, California, with his wife and two daughters.

In 1964, Jan and Dean were signed to host what became the first multi-act Rock and Roll show that was edited into a motion picture designed for wide distribution. *The T.A.M.I. Show* became a seminal and original production – in essence one of the first rock videos – on its release in 1964. Using a high-resolution videotape process called Electronovision (good enough to be transferred from television kinescope directly onto 35mm motion picture stock), new sound recording techniques and having a remarkable cast, *The T.A.M.I. Show* set the standard for all succeeding music film and video work, including many of the early videos shown by MTV 17 years later.

The revolutionary technical achievements of *The T.A.M.I. Show* and the legendary list of performers (including a performance by James Brown that many critics have called the best of his career) marked a high point for Jan and Dean, as they were the hosts and one of the main featured acts as well. They became one of the main faces of mid-1960s music, until Berry's auto accident two years later, through their *T.A.M.I. Show* appearance.

According to rock critic Dave Marsh, the attitude and public persona of punk rock can be traced to Jan and Dean. Certainly, their early hits, recorded with myriad overdubs in a garage, and their casual and goofy stage antics were consistent with some of punk rock's ethos. But their constant improvement and the increased complexity of their arrangements in the latter recordings showed their fealty to Brian Wilson's baroque approach.

Many of their records feature the top session players of the era, and their arrangements, with multiple key changes and complex vocal harmonies, reflected a high level of craftsmanship.

Nevertheless, Jan Berry and Dean Torrence's anti-establishment attitudes toward the music industry are well-documented. Their music has been covered by numerous punk rock and alternative rock bands since the 1970s.

Along with Phil Spector, Brian Wilson, and Lee Hazlewood, Berry enjoyed a reputation as one of the best record producers on the West Coast. Brian Wilson has cited Berry as having a direct impact on his own growth as a record producer.

In an interview conducted by Jan & Dean fan and historian David

Beard for the Collectors' Choice release, *Jan & Dean, the Complete Liberty Singles*, Dean Torrence stated that he felt the duo should be in the Rock & Roll Hall of Fame: "We have the scoreboard if you just want to compare number of hits and musical projects done. We beat 75-percent of the people in there.

So, what else is it? I've got to think that we were pretty irreverent when it came to the music industry. They kind of always held that against us. That's okay with me." Jan & Dean were however inducted into the Hollywood Rock Walk of Fame on April 12, 1996, exactly 30 years after Jan Berry had his near fatal car accident.

The Who covered Jan and Dean's song "Bucket T" on their UK EP 'Ready Steady Who' from 1966. It is one of only a few songs the group performed that Keith Moon (a huge surf music fan) provided the lead vocals.

Alternative rock group the *Red Hot Chili Peppers* referenced the duo in their song "Did I Let You Know", on the album *I'm With You*.

THE CHANTAYS

The Chantays are an American surf rock band from Orange County, California, known for the hit instrumental, "Pipeline" (1963). Their music combines electronic keyboards and surf guitar, creating a unique ghostly sound.

The Chantays were formed in 1961 when five high-school friends decided to start their own band. Bob Spickard, Brian Carman (co-writers of "Pipeline"), Bob Welch, Warren Waters and Rob Marshall were all students at Santa Ana High School in California, when a local group called the Rhythm Rockers inspired the five to form the Chantays.

In December 1962, the group recorded and released "Pipeline", which eventually peaked at No. 4 on the *Billboard* Hot 100 in May 1963. The track also peaked in the UK Singles Chart in 1963 at No. 16. The Chantays recorded their first album in 1963, also titled *Pipeline*, which included "Blunderbus" and "El Conquistador". Their follow-up album was *Two Sides of the Chantays* in 1964.

The Chantays toured Japan and the United States, joining *the Righ-*

teous Brothers and *Roy Orbison* on a few occasions, and they were the only rock and roll band to perform on The Lawrence Welk Show.

"Pipeline" (published as sheet music in 1962 by Downey Music Publishing) has become one of several surf rock hits. The tune has since been covered by Bruce Johnston, Welk (on the Dot album *Scarlet O'Hara*), Al Caiola (on the United Artists album *Greasy Kid Stuff*), the Ventures, Agent Orange, Hank Marvin, Lively Ones, Pat Metheny, Dick Dale with the help of Stevie Ray Vaughan (Grammy Nominated), by the thrash metal band Anthrax, Bad Manners, and Johnny Thunders. "Pipeline" has also been featured in many films, television programs and commercials. It also appears on numerous compilation albums.

The Chantays have been honored for their contributions to music. Some of the highlights include being honored on April 12, 1996 by Hollywood's Rock Walk, that was founded to honor individuals and bands that have made lasting and important contributions to music. "Pipeline" is listed as one of the 500 Songs that Shaped Rock and Roll. Along with Bill Medley of the Righteous Brothers and Diane Keaton, the Chantays were honored by the City of Santa Ana, California, and Santa Ana High School when they named a street after them, Chantays Way. OC Weekly Magazine also named the Chantays as one of the Best *Orange* County *Bands*.

Today, the Chantays are still playing. Original members Bob Spickard, Brian Carman, and Bob Welch were joined by longtime members Gil Orr, Ricky Lewis, and Brian Nussle. More recent albums include *The Next Set* (live recording) and *Waiting for the Tide*. Some of the tracks are new songs "Crystal T" and "Killer Dana", along with remakes of "Pipeline", "El Conquistador" and "Blunderbus".

Brian Carman died at his home in *Santa Ana*, California from complications of Crohn's disease on March 1, 2015. He was 69.

ALBUMS
Pipeline (1963)

THE BEL-AIRS

The Bel-Airs were an early and influential surf rock band from South Bay, Los Angeles, active in the early 1960s.

They were best known for their 1961 hit "Mr. Moto", an instrumental surf rock song that featured a flamenco-inspired intro and contained a melodic piano interlude. The song's theme was used in the solo for the song "Seed" by Sublime.

Upon splitting up, guitarist Eddie Bertrand formed Eddie & the Showmen in 1964, while guitarist Paul Johnson joined Cat Mother & the All Night Newsboys in 1970. Original Bel-Airs drummer Dick Dodd joined Bertrand in Eddie & the Showmen, and later joined the Standells, playing drums and singing lead on their major 1966 hit, "Dirty Water". Richard Delvy replaced Dick Dodd on drums and went on to found the surf group the Challengers.

Johnson has continued in music, both in recording and as a performer. Among other music associations, he has been a member of the "Jim Fuller version" of the Surfaris since 1990. Bertrand also continued in music, touring as Eddie and the Soundwaves, among other performance configurations. Dodd has participated in various reunions and later recordings of the Standells.

Eddie Bertrand died of cancer in November 2012.

Band Members

Eddie & the Showmen were an American surf rock band of the 1960s. Formed in Southern California by Eddie Bertrand, formerly of The Bel-Airs, they released several singles on Liberty Records. Their highest-charting single in Los Angeles was "Mr. Rebel", which reached No. 4 on the Wallichs Music City Hit List on February 10, 1964.

• The band originally formed because Bertrand wanted to move on from the Bel-Airs. While the Bel-Airs focused more on guitar interplay, and a moderate sound, Eddie & the Showmen played more in the style of Dick Dale with a prominent lead guitar and heavy sound. The band's original drummer was former Mousketeer Dick Dodd, who later joined

127

The Standells. One of the guitar players Larry Carlton later became a famous jazz guitarist, and another was Rob Edwards of Colours who was the guitarist on the title track for the surf movie, *Pacific Vibrations*.

• One of Eddie & the Showmen's biggest hits, "Squad Car", was a cover version of the Bel-Airs track. Eddie and the Showmen are included in the *Hard Rock Cafe: Surf* 1998 compilation of surf bands and surf music on track 11. *Mr. Rebel*. They are also included in *The Birth of Surf* compilation track 20 *Squad Car* and are on 10 tracks of *Toes on The Nose: 32 Surf Age Instrumentals* compilation.

• Eddie Bertrand died of cancer in November 2012.

THE SURFARIS SURF ROCK BAND

The Surfaris were an American surf rock band formed in Glendora, California in 1962. They are best known for two songs that hit the charts in the Los Angeles area, and nationally by May 1963: "Surfer Joe" and "Wipe Out", which were the A-side and B-side of a 45 rpm single.

The original band members were Ron Wilson (drums, vocals), Jim Fuller (lead guitar), Bob Berryhill (rhythm guitar) and Pat Connolly (bass).

In the fall of 1962, Southern California high school students Jim Fuller and Pat Connolly called friend and guitarist Berryhill for a practice session at Berryhill's house. The trio practiced for about 4 hours and met drummer Wilson at a high school dance later that evening, whereupon the band was born. "Wipe Out" was written and recorded by the quartet later that winter, with the song reaching #2 nationally in 1963 before becoming an international hit.

Saxophone player Jim Pash joined after their "Wipe Out" / "Surfer Joe" recording sessions at Pal Studios. Ken Forssi, later of Love, played bass with The Surfaris after Pat Connolly.

Wilson's energetic drum solo made "Wipe Out" one of the best-remembered instrumental songs of the period. "Wipe Out" is also remembered particularly for its introduction. Before the music starts, Berryhill's dad broke a board (imitating a breaking surfboard) near the mic, followed by a maniacal laugh and the words "Wipe Out" spoken by band manager Dale Smallin. "Wipe Out" was written in the studio by the four original members (Berryhill, Connolly, Fuller, & Wilson) and was originally going to be titled "Switchblade". It sold over one million copies and was awarded a gold disc.

The band released a series of records, with two other singles, "Surfer Joe" (written and sung by Wilson) and "Point Panic" (another group-composed instrumental), having an impact on the charts. Point Panic is a renowned surfing venue in Hawaii after which the song was named.

The original 1963 membership remained intact until August 1965 when Connolly departed before their Japanese tour. Ken Forssi replaced him on bass for the tour. Fuller resigned after the tour and the band folded in early 1966.

The group has periodically reunited and are still active, performing and recording, often re-recording their old and new songs. Drummer Ron Wilson died on 12 May 1989, one month short of his 45th birthday. Wilson had released an album of his songs, entitled *Lost It in The Surf*, on Bennet House Records of Grass Valley, California, which was recorded in June 1987.

A very small number of cassettes of this album were produced. *Lost It in the Surf* included a cover of "Louie Louie", complete with Scottish bagpipes. Forssi died from a brain tumor in 1998, and Pash died from heart failure in 2005.

Bob Berryhill currently performs under the Surfaris banner as "Bob Berryhill's Surfaris." Jim Fuller currently plays with his own band, "Jim Fuller and the Beatnik." Connolly has since left the music business.

"Wipe Out" hoax: Following the death of television personality *Morton Downey, Jr.*, news reports and obituaries incorrectly credited him as the composer of "Wipe Out" (as well as *The Chantays'* "Pipeline"). As of 2010, Downey's official website continued to make this claim but it has been changed to state he "also played major roles in the production of the hit surf music era songs Pipeline and Wipeout.

DICK DALE (SURFING MUSIC STYLE PIONEER)

Dick Dale (born Richard Anthony Monsour on May 4, 1937) is an American surf rock guitarist, known as The King of the Surf Guitar. He pioneered the surf music style, drawing on Eastern musical scales and experimenting with reverberation. He worked closely with Fender to produce custom made amplifiers, including the first-ever 100-watt guitar amplifier.

He pushed the limits of electric amplification technology, helping to develop new equipment that was capable of producing distorted, "thick, clearly defined tones" at "previously undreamed-of volumes." The "break-neck speed of his single-note staccato picking technique" and showman-ship with the guitar is considered a precursor to heavy metal music, influ-encing guitarists such as Jimi Hendrix and Eddie Van Halen.

Dale was born Richard Anthony Monsour in Boston, Massachusetts, on May 4, 1937, although many biographies of Dale repeat his earlier assertion that he was born in Beirut, Lebanon. He is of Lebanese descent from his father and Polish-Belarusian descent from his mother. His fa-ther was born in Beirut, and his mother's parents came to the U.S. from Poland; they farmed in Whitman, Massachusetts.

Dale's family moved to Quincy, Massachusetts, which had a signif-icant Lebanese immigrant community, when Dale was very young. He learned to play music, starting with piano when he was nine.

Dale admired Hank Williams—he wanted to be a cowboy singer—so he bought a plastic ukulele for $6 and taught himself to play by reading an instruction book. The first song he played on the ukulele was Tennessee Waltz. He then learned to play guitar, using a combination style incorpo-rating both lead and rhythm aspects, so that the guitar filled the place of drums.

He was raised in Quincy until he completed the 11th grade at Quincy High School in 1954, when his machinist father obtained a job in the Southern California aerospace industry. His parents drove the family across the country to live in El Segundo, California.

Dale spent his senior year at and graduated from Washington Senior High School. It was in Southern California that he learned to surf at the age of 17. He soon learned to play the drums and the trumpet. Due to his Lebanese heritage, he also had a strong interest in Arabic music, which later played a major role in his development of surf rock music.

Among his early musical influences was his uncle. According to Dale, "My uncle taught me how to play the tarabaki, and I watched him play the oud. We used to play at the Maharjan [an annual Lebanese festival in Greater Boston] while relative's belly-danced." His early tarabaki drumming later influenced his guitar playing, particularly his rapid alternating picking technique.

According to Dale, "It's the pulsation," stating that whether he is playing the guitar, trumpet, or piano, "They all have that drumming beat I learned by playing the tarabaki."

Dale is credited as one of the first electric guitarists to employ fast scales in his playing. Dale was a surfer and wanted his music to reflect the sounds he heard in his mind while surfing. He was among the first guitarists to use reverb—which gave the guitar a "wet" sound that has become a staple of surf music.

Dale's staccato picking, however, is his trademark. Being left-handed, he initially had to play a right-handed guitar, but then changed to a left-handed model. However, he did so without restringing the guitar, leading him to effectively play the guitar upside-down (Hendrix, for example, restrung his guitar), often playing by reaching over the fretboard rather than wrapping his fingers up from underneath.

Dale is also noted for playing his percussive, heavy bending style, using what most guitarists consider very heavy gauge strings (16p, 18p, 20p. 38w, 48w, 58w guitar string manufacturers do not make string sets for standard tuned electric guitars heavier than 13 to 56).

His desire to create a certain sound led him to push the limits of equipment.

Leo Fender kept giving Dale amps and Dale kept blowing them up! Till one night Leo and his right hand man Freddy T. (Freddie Tavares) went down to the Rendezous Ballroom on the Balboa Peninsula in Balboa, California and stood in the middle of four thousand screaming and dancing Dick Dale fans, and said to Freddie, I now know what Dick Dale is trying to tell me.

They went to James B. Lansing loudspeaker company and explained that they wanted a fifteen -inch loudspeaker built to their specifications.

131

The unit became famous as the 15" JBL D130F model.

It made the complete package for Dale to play through and was named the Single Showman Amp. When Dale plugged his Fender Stratocaster guitar into the new Showman Amp and loudspeaker cabinet, Dale became the first person on earth to jump from the volume scale of a modest quiet guitar player (on a scale of 4) to blasting up through the volume scale to Ten! That is when Dale became the "Father of Heavy Metal" as quoted from *Guitar Player* magazine. Dale broke through the electronic barrier limitations of that era!

During a six-month period that began July 1, 1961, Dale's performances at the Rendezvous Ballroom in Balboa are credited with the creation of the surf music phenomenon. Dale asked for and gained permission to use the 3,000 person capacity ballroom for surfer dances after overcrowding at a local ice cream parlor where he performed made him seek other venues.

The Rendezvous ownership and the city of Newport Beach agreed to Dale's request on the condition that he prohibit alcohol sales and implement a dress code. Dale's events at the ballrooms, called "stomps," quickly became legendary, and the events routinely sold out. Paul Johnson, guitarist for the contemporary group The Bel-Airs, recalled the electric atmosphere of the shows:

I remember making the trek to the Rendezvous in the summer of '61 to see what all the fuss was about over Dick Dale. It was a powerful experience; his music was incredibly dynamic, louder and more sophisticated than The Belairs, and the energy between The Del-Tones and all of those surfers stomping on the hardwood floor in their sandals was extremely intense. The tone of Dale's guitar was bigger than any I had ever heard, and his blazing technique was something to behold.

Let's Go Trippin' is often regarded as the first Surf Rock song. This was followed by more locally released songs, including Jungle Fever and Surf Beat on his own Deltone label. His first full-length album was Surfers' Choice in 1962. The album was picked up by Capitol Records and distributed nationally, and Dale soon began appearing on The Ed Sullivan Show, and in films where he played his signature single Misirlou.

He later stated, "I still remember the first night we played it ("Misirlou"). I changed the tempo, and just started cranking on that mother. And...it was eerie. The people came rising up off the floor, and they were chanting and stomping. I guess that was the beginning of the surfer's stomp." His second album was named after his performing nickname, King of the Surf Guitar.

Dick Dale and the Dell-tones performed the songs "My First Love," "Runnin' Wild" and "Muscle Beach" in the 1964 film, Muscle Beach Party.

Dale and the Del-Tones performed both sides of his Capitol single, Secret Surfin' Spot / Surfin' and Swingin' in the popular 1963 movie, Beach Party, starring Frankie Avalon and Annette Funicello. This helped bring Dick Dale, surf music, and surf culture to national prominence.

He also appeared in the 1987 film, back to the Beach—in which Avalon's character, reluctant to attend a Dick Dale concert, remarks to Funicello, "We can come back here in the year 2000 and see Dick!"—a testimony to Dale's continued popularity and career longevity.

Surf rock's national popularity was somewhat brief, as the British Invasion began to overtake the American charts in 1964. Though he continued performing live, Dale was soon set back by rectal cancer. In the liner notes of Better Shred Than Dead: The Dick Dale Anthology, the thought, "Then you'll never hear surf music again," was Jimi Hendrix's reaction upon hearing that Dale had a possibly terminal case of colon cancer, intended to encourage his comrade to recuperate.

Dale, in gratitude to his late friend, later covered Third Stone from the Sun as a tribute to Hendrix. Though he recovered, he retired from music for several years. In 1979, he almost lost a leg after being injured while swimming and a pollution-related infection made the mild injury much worse.

As a result, Dale became an environmental activist and soon began performing again. He recorded a new album in 1986 and was nominated for a Grammy. In 1987 he appeared in the movie Back to the Beach, playing surf music and performing Pipeline with Stevie Ray Vaughan.

In 1993, he recorded a guitar solo on the track Should Have Known on a vinyl single by a Southern California indie band, The Pagodas. The use of Misirlou in the 1994 Quentin Tarantino film Pulp Fiction gained him a new audience.

In 1995, he recorded a surf-rock version of Camille Saint-Saëns's *Aquarium* from *The Carnival of the Animals* for the musical score of the enclosed roller coaster, Space Mountain at Disneyland in Anaheim, California. In 1997, Dale appeared in the campy cult film *An American Vampire Story*, performing a rousing guitar solo on the beach with his son on drums. In 2002, Dale appeared in *The True Meaning of Christmas Specials*, playing several original songs for the program.

The National Hockey League's Colorado Avalanche use Dale's song *Scalped* as their theme song. The Black Eyed Peas' song *Pump It* (from the 2005 album *Monkey Business*) heavily samples Dale's *Misirlou*. *Misirlou* also features in the PlayStation 2/Xbox 360 video game, Guitar Hero II, as well as the Wii video game Rayman Raving Rabbids.

In the feature film Space Jam, as Elmer Fudd and Yosemite Sam (in a parody of the Pulp Fiction characters Vincent Vega and Jules Winnfield) shoot out teeth from one of the Monstars, a clip from Misirlou plays.

In 2009, he was inducted into the Musicians Hall of Fame and Museum in Nashville, TN. Dale is also a 2011 inductee into the Surfing Walk of Fame in Huntington Beach, California, in the Surf Culture category.

Dale said in the 1990s that he was not born in Beirut, Lebanon, as he had been telling interviewers for decades. He said he was born in Boston.

Dale has said that he has never used alcohol or other drugs and discourages their use by band members and road crew. Health was a priority for him. In 1972, he stopped eating red meat. He studied martial arts for over 30 years. At age 78 he is still putting on physically energetic live shows. In early 2008, he experienced a recurrence of rectal cancer and finished a surgical, chemotherapy, and radiation treatment regimen.

In June, 2009 Dale began a West Coast tour from Southern California to British Columbia, with approximately 20 concert dates. "Forever Came Calling" (or FCC) featured Dale's then-17-year-old son, Jimmy Dale on drums, who opened for him. He was scheduled to play the Australian One Great Night On Earth festival to raise funds to benefit those affected by the Black Saturday bushfires and other natural disasters. Dale continues to perform at venues across the U.S. into 2015 in order to pay for medical bills.

In addition to Fender amplifiers, Dale is associated with the Fender Stratocaster guitar. Fender makes a signature model, the Dick Dale Custom Shop Stratocaster, fitted with "Custom Shop '54" pickups and intended to recreate the sound of the first Stratocaster. Dale used a reverb unit with the signal split between two Fender Dual Showman amps.

As of 2010, Dale continued to play with his original reverb unit and Showman amps from the early 1960s, continuing his practice of stringing his left-handed guitar upside down. The unique features of this guitar include a toggle switch that bypasses the three-position blade switch to activate neck and middle pickups only.

Albums
Surfers' Choice (Deltone 1962)
King of the Surf Guitar (Capitol 1963)

Soundtracks
Pulp Fiction Soundtrack (MCA 1994)

Peel Sessions
Peel later selected *Let's Go Trippin'* as the theme tune for his BBC Radio 4 series *Home Truths*.

THIRTEEN

—

CHARLIE GOT AN EMAIL from Greg Irvine (the Mayor of the city of Irvine) in the OC (Orange County). Then just a few minutes later he got another email from the State Assembly woman who represents Irvine in Sacramento. Both emails said basically the same thing, and that was, large Marijuana fields were found way up in the foothills of the 'Orange County Great Park'. They were located in a very desolate area in the North East side of the park where no one ever goes.

A tourist at the Park was taking one of the fabulous and very popular Hot Air Balloon (Aerophile SA) rides. As they glided over the Park which had a marvelous view of the lovely blue Pacific Ocean, he looked down and spotted what he thought looked like hundreds of Marijuana, or Hemp, plants.

The Park is 4,682 acres and a lot of it is still undeveloped do to the poor economy the past several years. It was started after the closing of the old El Toro Marine Corp Air Station several years ago.

The Great *Recession* (2007-2013) was in Charlie's opinion in reality the second Great *Depression*, (First 1929-1934) and not a recession at all. He has a B/A Degree in Economics from the wonderful California State University-Fullerton in the OC as well as his B/A Degree in Criminal Justice from the same school. The Recession, or Depression, whatever you chose to call it, was the reason for the OC Great Park to still be largely undeveloped.

When the Park was informed of the possible Marijuana fields by the sharp-eyed visitor, they immediate called in the IPD (Irvine Police Department) to investigate who was growing illegal Pot in their State Park. When they were unable to identify who planted the groves, the IPD, called in the very efficient Orange County Sheriff's Department.

The OC Sheriff (Sandra) was a close friend of Charlie's and he had worked with her when they were both employed at the LAPD (Los Angeles Police Department). They were both assigned back in the day as detective Lieutenant's at the departments infamous Rampart Division located close to MacArthur Park, right downtown LA.

The quite large camp site was deserted by the time the IPD, and the OC Sheriff's, got there, of course. The drug growers obviously had scouts nearby at all times to warn them if any cops came calling. Charlie and Sandra personally and very carefully examined the site. She had her department burn and destroy all of the Marijuana crop.

She told Charlie the pot stash left behind by the drug dealers was worth about three Million dollars. The growers had left it all as they ran for their lives, so to speak, as the Police made their raid on the fields.

Then the very sharp and efficient law enforcement OC Sheriff, told Charlie that recently several very large Marijuana 'grows' had been located in the Natural Forests and County Parks throughout Orange County, mostly during the past 12 months. And, she wanted Charlie, and his Angels, to find out if at all possible, if they were just local drug growers/ dealers, or if they were part of an international Mexican Drug Cartel.

Sandra confided in Charlie that do to several recent large department budget cuts, she just did not have the extra detectives to work on this case at the present time. She also added that there had been a rash of recent Bank robberies, as well as Murders, in Orange County recently.

Charlie told his good friend, Sandra, not to worry and that he and his Angels would find out who the perps were as soon as possible, and then added that it was great to be working with her again. Almost like the good ole days in LA.

Next Charlie called his good buddy, Howard, at the CIA in Langley, Virginia, and asked for his help *again*. Charlie thought Howard must be 'sick and tired' of him always asking for assistances on his investigations, but then he realized that Howard would just tell him, "No problem, my old PI friend."

Charlie hoped that someday he would be able to show his appreciation to Howard for all of his help on his PI cases over the years and also for saving his bacon (life) many, many times.

Charlie asked Howard to have his people at the CIA, and also his good friend at the FBI, to see if they could dig up any useful information about pot growers/dealers operating out of Orange County, California. It was a long shot; however, Charlie knew that they had lots more resources than he did, and also, they could use some old and new Satellite images of the Park. And those photos could be quite helpful, indeed.

Next Charlie called his three Angels, Letty, Gabby, and Lulu, and asked them to meet him for lunch at the world-famous Balboa Bay Yacht Club located inside the lovely Newport Bay Harbor. He wanted to tell them about their new assignment of looking into the deserted Pot Farm and who planted and cultivated it, right in the OC Great Park.

After a fabulous lobster and steak lunch with his Team, then he called his good amigo, Manny Murrieta, in Tijuana. He asked Manny if he could assist with the investigation, and Manny said, "Good to hear from you PI buddy, and sure always glad to help an old amigo, I will be on the next flight out of TJ and be at the John Wayne Airport in three hours."

Charlie felt that Manny would be a great asset to his case since he used to work with the DEA (i.e. Drug Enforcement Agency) in both the OC, California as well as Baja California, Mexico. Also, Manny, had a great deal of knowledge about drug dealers, sellers, marijuana growers, and the Mexican Drug Cartels who operate inside of the California border.

The Orange County Great Park is the official name of a plan for the public, non-aviation reuse of the decommissioned Marine Corps Air Station El Toro in Irvine, California. The county park will comprise just 28.8% (1,347 acres (5.45 km^2)) of the 4,682 acres (18.95 km^2) total that made up the old MCAS El Toro base. It is a $1.1 billion project approved by the voters of Orange County in 2002.

Initial proposals after the retirement of the Marine Corps Air Station included an international airport, possible housing and the great park. In 2001, Orange County voters passed "Measure W" authorizing the former air station's use as a Central Park/Nature Preserve and multi-use development. The measure was passed, which led to the designation of the land as the OC Great Park.

The closing of MCAS El Toro ignited a political firestorm over the eventual fate of the facility. With its existing infrastructure, some favored converting the base into an international airport. Those favoring the new airport tended to come from northern *Orange County,* (desiring the convenience of a closer airport), and from areas in Newport Beach that are within the arrival and departure noise zones surrounding John Wayne Airport, (hoping to close that airport in favor of the new one at El Toro).

Those against the airport proposal were largely residents of the cities in the immediate vicinity of El Toro, such as Irvine, Lake Forest, Laguna Niguel, Laguna Woods, Dana Point, and Mission Viejo, where residents were alarmed at the idea of the aircraft noise.

The cities opposed to the airport created a joint powers authority, the El Toro Reuse Planning Authority (ETRPA) to oppose the project. They were joined in the effort by grass-roots organizations that collected record numbers of signatures on petitions to place anti-airport initiatives on the ballot and raised funds for the election campaigns.

In 2002, after lengthy debate that lasted for over a dozen years, Orange County voters rejected the commercial airport plan and designated the land for park compatible uses.

The re-use of the air station was voted on by the residents of Orange County four times. In March 2000, opponents of the airport were able to qualify for the ballot "Measure F," which required that any new construction of jails, landfills or airports would require a 2/3 majority vote. A resounding 67.3% of voters passed Measure F, effectively killing the potential airport project.

In 2001, Orange County voters passed "Measure W" authorizing the former air station's use as a Central Park/Nature Preserve and multi-use development. The measure passed with 58% of the vote due to the lack of any other viable alternatives for the former site since the airport concept was effectively killed a year earlier. The history of the controversy is chronicled online by the El Toro Info Site.

In November 2003, the city of Irvine annexed the air station property and was thus able to determine the Great Park's future by zoning.

Following the annexation of the property, the Department of the Navy held an online auction for the El Toro property. Miami- based Lennar Corporation purchased the entire property for $649,500,000 and entered into a development agreement with the City of Irvine. Under the terms of the development agreement, Lennar was granted limited development rights to build the Great Park Neighborhoods in return for land and capital that will allow the construction of the Great Park.

The agreement required Lennar to deed 1,347 acres (5.45 km²) to public ownership and contribute $200 million towards the development of the Great Park. Future property owners will contribute an additional $200 million toward the park's development.

The Great Park Plan focuses on the 1,347 acres (5.45 km²) public of the property and includes a 2.5-mile (4.0 km) canyon, a 26-acre (110,000 m²) lake. At 1,347 acres (5.45 km²), the Great Park will be larger than New York's Central Park, San Francisco's Golden Gate Park and San Diego's Balboa Park.

When completed, the park will be the largest municipal park in Orange County. The original plan for the infrastructure of the Great Park was virtually identical to Newport Center, with five roads connecting into a central loop road separating the park into "blocks".

The design was later modified to include a large section of runway and conform more to the layout of the original base, as a reminder of its history. Most prominent in the park plans is the restoration of Agua Chinon Creek, which had been channeled underground ever since the base was built in the 1940s.

Recently however, in the midst of a U.S. housing crisis, Lennar has struggled to fulfill its part of the bargain, including delayed construction of planned housing and of a 'community facilities district'. In addition to trees that will be moved and replanted on the base, Southern California Edison has committed to contributing 50,000 trees to the Great Park.

The Canyon was voted by Irvine City Council on July 17th, 2014 for removal from the Great Park plan. Five Point Communities was also given approval for 4,606 more homes near the park in exchange for $200 million to develop 688 acres of the park which will include golf courses, a sports park and nature trails.

All of the usual suspects: Charlie found a good possible suspect with a 'little help' from his friend Howard at the CIA who had got a hot tip from his friend at the FBI (in Quantico, Virginia).

Through very detailed Spy satellite images (amazing how clear a picture from outer space can be, Charlie said to himself), they could see when the grow first started last year. There were dozens and dozens of construction vehicles, both big and small, coming and going for several months to the far back reaches of the Great OC Park.

Charlie then added, "I cannot believe that with all of that activity, no one noticed nor reported, anything to the Irvine PD?" The images also provided very helpful details and numbers from the license plates on the work vehicles. By tracing those numbers, the FBI was able to track them back to the 'White Rulers'.

They were a west coast branch of a quite large degenerate Skin Head group from Atlanta, Georgia. That main group called themselves the 'White World Domination' party.

The leader of the White Rulers name was Manfred 'Calhoun' Chambers and he lived out in the IE (Inland Empire) with the rest of his drug growing/dealing skin head gang. He lived in the city of Parris, not that far from the OC Park, actually, just down the 15 (Las Vegas) Freeway south to the 405 (San Diego) and then north.

Perris was a very nice, quaint little town of mostly retired people out in the Simi-desert and close to Murrieta and Temecula. For some unknown reason, however, loser skin heads groups and renegade motorcycle gangs loved to live out there. Very few police and the local Sheriff's office and the California Highway Patrol were seldom in that area.

Calhoun as he preferred to be called (or our supreme leader) according to FBI records, was a Stone Cold and merciless killer. He was also a heavy meth (methamphetamine) user and had been a drug day tripper for years. Also, associates of his told the FBI that he was a 'ticking time bomb' with a lit fuse and just waiting to explode at any given minute.

Also, it was said that Calhoun had crystal clear blue eyes and were brooding and quite sinister. And they never stopped moving from left to right and right to left. He had been shot, and also knifed, several times before and he was always on the ready for an attack at anytime. He had clearly sold his soul to the Devil, that was obvious to Charlie.

Lastly, the confidential FBI reports said that Calhoun was deeply in debt to his crazy leaders in Atlanta (Hot Lanta as some call it) and he needed a lot of money to pay them as well as support his skin head gang (of about 50 members plus their biker mama's and kids, about 100 all together) a lot of mouths to feed, and all of that heavy financial burden not to even mention, support his several thousand dollar a week meth habit. A Great prospect for the hemp field bad guy.

More suspects, Charlie's three Angels, namely Letty, Gabby, and Lulu (whom were working all together this time) had found out through some CI's (Confidential Informants) that an outlaw motor cycle gang called the 'Monguls' was big, real big, into marijuana grow farms.

Especially in the National parks in Riverside and San Bernardino counties and also the OC (Orange County). The Monguls' MC gang (AKA the Mongul Nation or the Mongul Brotherhood) was founded in East LA (Los Angeles, California) way back in 1969.

The President was William 'Billy' St. John, Vice President Robert Fink and Sergeant of Arms was James 'Stomper' Christopher. They have been notorious rivals of the quite infamous 'Hells Angels' since their inception and still to this very day.

Law Enforcement agencies from all over the United States, estimate that there are about 1,000 to 1,500 Full Patch members, with the expansion to Australia in 2015. They have chapters in 14 States as well as international chapters in 13 foreign countries., mainly in Europe.

The agencies also say that the outlaw biker gang, is suspected of: heavy involvement with the illegal Drug Trade growing and selling marijuana, money laundering, robbery, extortion, protection, murder, firearms violations, assault amongst many, many other heinous crimes.

Charlie told Manny and his Angels, that Christopher was a good candidate for the Grow Farm since he was in charge of bringing in extra money for the MC gang, as well as dishing out punishment for members whom do not follow their strict code of conduct. It was reported that he loved meeting out punishment, truly loved it. He was a psychopath through and through, Charlie said.

Even more suspects, Manny narrowed his search for a guilt party down to either the infamous Sinaloa Drug Cartel (centered in Tijuana, Mexico) Or the Tecate Drug Cartel (who operated out of Tecate, Mexico). They were both competitors for the very lucrative drug trade and people smuggling, along the US and Mexico in Baja California. Both Cartels smuggled illegals from Mexico, Lots from South America (El Salvador, Honduras, and Guatemala, Europe, and recently many from the Middle East. This caused the US government great worry, to say the least.

Their drug Wars over the years had killed, or seriously injured, hundreds and hundreds of Cartel members as well as thousands of good and innocent Mexican citizens. Citizens whom according to Charlie, "Were just in the wrong place and at the wrong time."

Manny also told Charlie, that there was a small possibility that the EPR (Ejecito Popular Revolucionario) might be involved as they were short of capital that they needed for their desired overthrow of the legitimate Mexican government. Manny, then added, "Charlie I think that it is unlikely that the EPR would come this far north, cross the US Border, and would want to fight a Turf War over a marijuana grow with either the Sinaloa, or the Tecate Drug Cartels. Very unlikely."

SUSPECT SUMMARY LIST

One: Manfred 'Calhoun' Chambers (White Rulers)
Two: James 'Stomper' Christopher (Monguls Brotherhood)
Three: Sinaloa Drug Cartel (Tijuana, Mexico)
Four: Tecate Drug Carte (Tecate, Mexico)
and last but certainly not least,
Five: The EPR (Mexico City, Mexico)

Charlie told Manny and his Angels, that there could be other possible perp's (perpetrators and/or guilty parties) other than these, however, after a lot of investigation by the CIA, the FBI, the DEA, as well as themselves, it was quite unlikely. Unlikely indeed.

Just as Charlie, and his bonita (beautiful in Spanish) three Private Eye Angels, were about to solve the Pot farm mystery at the 'Great OC Park', he got a secure and encrypted satellite cell phone call from his good amigo Howard at the CIA. Howard told Charlie that he had to come to Washington DC, soon. Then in mid-sentence he said "No, I do not mean soon, I mean get your butt on the next non-stop flight out of the John Wayne Airport (in Irvine, California)."

Then Howard went on to tell Charlie that he was needed to testify at a top-secret session of a Congressional Senate sub-committee in DC. And added that the closed-door meeting was for the purpose of investigating the recent increase of criminal activity of Mexican Drug Cartel's along both sides of the US and Mexican border.

Mainly the area from the Pacific Ocean (just south of lovely San Diego, California) and all the way due East to the Colorado River in Arizona.

Also, Howard added that because of Charlie's recent experience, and successful rescue of Thomas Rose (the Chairman of the Board of Directors as well as the CEO-Chief Executive Officer, of 'The Bank of Orange County') and his quite successful and knowledgeable wife (Pamela).

That rescue had involved the very large and well-organized Sinaloa Drug Cartel, which operates out of the lovely little tourist town of Tijuana, Mexico, in Baja California.

In addition, Howard said the sub-committee was also quite interested in Charlie's current investigation with a large Marijuana Grow in the foothills of the 'Great OC Park' (in El Toro), in the OC (Orange County), California. That Pot farm might, just possibly, in their opinion be linked to a Mexican Drug Cartel.

Then, our man Charlie told Howard, "when the US Government calls, I am there. Tell the committee chairwoman (Janet Russell) that I will be in Washington, DC in eight hours of less." Charlie was quite honored that the Senate of the United States of America wanted to hear from him and get his opinion on the Cartel's recent rise in growing, and smuggling drugs into the US. The only problem for Charlie, and it was a major one indeed, was that he would have to put his current and very important investigation into his case about the Hemp farm, on hold until he returned from DC.

Charlie then asked his wonderful Angels to keep *digging* into the possible perp's in this case and also to try to find out if there were any more suspects that they may have missed the first time around in their investigation.

All three Angels were top notch Private Eyes and very knowledgeable about criminal activity and Drug growing and selling Mexican Cartel's. Especially in the Baja California area.

Charlie, therefore, was not afraid to leave them alone to work this crucial investigation while he was in the Nation's Capital (Washington, DC). Can you imagine Charlie said to himself, "The US Government wants to talk, face to face, with me? Will wonders never cease." Then he smiled, a big proud smile.

Then Charlie told Letty, Gabby, and Lulu (his precious PI Angels) that he would call them on their cell phones, email to their cells, or text them for updates on the Pot farm investigation at the end of each day that he was in DC. Then he added that he would be back in the OC as soon as possible.

He then promised his Angels that if they had not solved the case, for the great city of Irvine and the wonderful and efficient OC Sheriff's Department (and the good Sheriff herself) before he returned, that they would solve it together. Then added one of his favorite sayings, "And you can take that to the Bank."

When Charles boarded his non-stop flight from the John Wayne Airport to the Washington/Baltimore International Thurgood Marshall Airport in Washington DC, he noted that it was a brand-new Boeing 737. He is a PI you know. Also, he noticed to his quite pleasant surprise, that there were three absolutely 'drop dead' gorgeous flight attendants to greet the passengers.

Charlie then noted that their name tags read Jan, Susan (Sue) and Sharon (Shari). Once again, he does not miss much and as I already have stated, he is a Private Detective.

Jan was quite tall 5'8", lovely long legs (and as you already know Charlie is a leg man), great figure athletic and well toned, brunette with auburn highlights, very nice highlights, very pretty as well as a little bit mysterious dark brown eyes, he loved her eyes, a lot. Later during the flight as she joined him in his last in the row seat at the back of the plane, there was an empty seat next to him, what a break for him, he said to himself and then smiled.

She told Charlie that she had a pretty sister named Lynn who lived in the OC. Also, that she loved to dance and wondered if Charlie would like to take her dancing when they got to DC.

There she had a three day lay over with nothing to do, poor little thing Charlie thought. Perhaps he may just be able to come to her rescue, you know he is so helpful with a woman in distress. Especially one whom was so adorable and charming too.

Then Charlie after a three second delay said, "I would be delighted to take you out to dinner and then dancing when we get there." Then he asked her, "Jan, do you know how to country-western two-step?" To which she responded, I just love to two steps, I am from Tucson, Arizona you know." He felt like it was not going to be just all business in DC, for which he was well please, indeed.

Next there was Sue, she had quite lovely long blonde hair down to her slim waist, 5'2" with eyes of blue, naturally. Later in the flight she told Charlie that she had been a surfer chick when she was younger and used to hang out at the Huntington State Beach pier in Surf City USA (Huntington Beach, California). And that she could surf as good as the guys, and better than a lot. From the look of her body, Charlie did not find that hard to believe, at all.

Then there was Shari, and she was a pretty redhead about 5'4" quite lovely face and body features, but like Charlie, just a few pounds overweight. She was quite friendly to Charlie, and he thought that she might be a little bit sweet on him.

After meeting all three very lovely flight attendants, and after a very brief chat with each of them, Charlie said to himself, not out loud of course, "Charlie your lucky old dog, this is going to be a marvelous flight and it is clearly *not* going to be boring like your normal plane trips".

After those exciting conversations, the new 737 jet plane was up in the air looking down on Charlie's beloved Orange County and the royal blue Pacific Ocean. And then, in a blink of his mysterious hazel eyes, and in a heartbeat, and in a split second, Charlie said, "Hasta la vista" (Goodbye) to the OC (Orange County) and then our man, Charlie was gone!

ACKNOWLEDGEMENTS

Howard, my good friend, he loves the cold and snow of Minnesota, even though he is from sunny southern California. And David Alan (my great son) who is more intelligent than I am, my Hero, and his successful and wife Desiree'. Also, to her nice parents Cesar and Yolanda. And the best granddaughter in the world, Morgan Marie.

Betty, my adopted mother who is also one on my most dedicated readers. She just loves my 'Charlie' the Private Investigator. My sister Jan who is a gracious and kind poet and her husband John and their three cool cats. My quite intelligent other sister Lisa, her husband Professor Bob and their two neat rescue dogs. And, Jan my mother-in-Law and excellent novel reviewer, she is the best.

Leann, John, Lindsay, and Zach. Dr. Anne, the best doctor in Orange County. Monja, Tammy, and Richard of the terrific Laguna Café. Best food and service in town. And my great bankers Jason, Mehrnaz, Christine, and Vincent.

The excellent OCSD Sheriff, Sandra Hutchens. And, Brad Hudson, CEO, and Teresa of VMS. My good friends, Brother Thomas and Pamela, Jim and Betty best neighbors ever, and, Brett Long my terrific DC. And Mary and Carol.

Also, and my good friends, Janey 'Sunshine' Dorrell and Juanita Skillman of United Mutual.

And Wayne and Donna Leicht who own and operate the wonderous" Kristalle" (Minerals and Gold Specimens) business in lovely Laguna Beach.

And, last but certainly not least, my humble 'Thank you' to all of my good readers. And, also my sincere apologies to anyone who I have 'accidentally' forgotten to acknowledge, in this section of my novel.